Evernight Publishing

www.evernightpublishing.com

SAM CRESCENT

Copyright© 2015

Sam Crescent

Editor: Karyn White

Cover Artist: Sour Cherry Designs

Jacket Design: Jay Aheer

ISBN: 978-1-77233-506-4

ALL RIGHTS RESERVED

BETRAYAL

DEDICATION

I want to thank my readers for their continued support and love of my work. To Evernight and my wonderful editor, Karyn. You're all amazing to work with.

BETRAYAL

BETRAYAL

Trojans MC, 2

Sam Crescent

Copyright © 2015

Prologue

"What are you doing here?" Mary asked, opening the door to find Pike waiting.

"Do I need a reason to come and see you?" He brushed past her going straight to the kitchen. Holly had left over twenty minutes ago, and Mary had expected to be alone. She loved her friend, but there were times she did like to have some alone time to get her focus on the world around her. Their apartment was small and she enjoyed baking with Holly, but her real passion was creating recipes for a book of her own. Working in the diner wasn't challenging to her, especially when all she did was take orders and watch Mac cook. He didn't really know what he was doing. There was nothing inspiring about the recipes he created.

Closing the door behind Pike, she followed him down toward the kitchen where he was cutting himself a slab of pie.

"Holly's not here. She's gone out."

"It's okay. I'm not here to see Holly. I'd never be here to see her." He took a forkful of pie, closing his eyes.

Did he like it? She shouldn't care if he liked her food or not, yet it had been inbuilt in her to hope that Pike liked everything. For as long as she could remember Pike had been in her life, saving her when life got too hard at home. He was the one guy she'd always had a crush on, a stupid, immature crush that should be squashed down without any hope of it ever causing her a problem. She wasn't in love with him or anything. It was just a stupid crush that had her heart pounding whenever he was around. There was no way he'd ever go for a girl like her anyway. She'd seen the club whores he dated, and there was no way she'd ever really compare, not really.

At twenty-one she was still a damn virgin.

"Wow, you keep getting better and better."

Her cheeks heated under his compliment.

"Thank you." Gripping the back of her neck, she stared down the length of his body as he closed his eyes again to enjoy her pie. He was tall, well over six feet, and muscular. She'd watched him working out when she was at the clubhouse with Holly. Pike was a gorgeous, sexy man, and knew it as well. He was also a total whore. No woman stayed around for long with him. He fucked and left. She used to hear the women talking about him, betting on who would be able to snag him. None of them would. The only time Pike would ever settle down was when he decided, not a woman.

He turned and smiled at her. She looked away from his deep blue gaze, wishing there was something else to do.

"If you're not looking for Holly, why are you here?"

She wasn't under any illusions either. The club, the Trojans MC, only put up with her because of her friendship with Holly.

Pike stood behind her, pushing the hair off the back of her neck. Goosebumps erupted all over her skin. She'd never been touched so intimately before. Mary bit her lip to contain her moan. What kind of woman was she to be turned on by him simply moving hair off her neck?

"I don't need Holly to be here to want to be here, baby." One of his hands banded around her waist, pulling her against him. Closing her eyes, Mary didn't know what to do when she felt the evidence of his cock pressing against her ass. Mary had never been this close to him before.

"What are you doing?" she asked.

His lips brushed her neck, the rough bristles of his stubble turning her on even more.

"What's the matter, baby? I thought you wanted me."

This was not what she imagined. Swallowing past the lump in her throat she forced herself to open her eyes.

"You don't want me," she said.

He rubbed his cock against her ass. "Does this feel like a guy who doesn't want you? I want you, Mary. Ever since that pesky little ass of yours showed itself around the club. I'm not talking your girl ass or even your teenage ass—I'm talking about that woman's ass that is so full and round. Many guys think it's too big, but you know what I call them?" She shook her head, completely shocked by what was going on. "I call those men pussies. They're fucking boys in men's bodies. They don't know a good fucking ass when they see one. I see your ass, Mary. I see it, and I want to spank it, watch it bounce as it rides my cock, and I want to fuck it."

She gasped as his hand moved up to cup her breasts.

"Now, these tits, that's another matter. These I've imagined a hell of a lot. They're so big and ripe. They need to be fucked, sucked, and put on display. I want to watch them bounce as I fuck your sweet, virginal pussy, Mary."

"Pike, what are you doing?" she asked. Her pussy was dripping wet with her cream. In all the time she'd known Pike never once had he been alone with her. Was this the reason why? Why was he doing this now?

"I'm doing what the hell I want to. Is your little pussy wet for me, Mary? Do you want my dick to break through that virgin wall of yours?" He stroked her nipples, circling the hard buds as he licked across her collarbone. "Can't you answer me? I'll check for myself."

The hand on her waist moved down, sliding into the sweatpants she'd changed into when Holly left. She wasn't wearing any panties, and she listened to him groan against her neck.

"No panties and you're dripping. You're wetter than I ever imagined. Fuck, baby, I'm going to have this pussy tonight. I've spent a long time being good. It's time for us both to be very bad." He circled her clit, and Mary dropped her head back against his shoulder unable to hold herself up straight. "Yeah, you want it, and I'm going to be the one to give it to you."

She didn't fight him as he spun her around, withdrawing his hand from her pants. Pike brought his hand up to his face, inhaling the scent of her pussy from his fingers. A second later, he sucked the same fingers into his mouth.

"Your pussy is so fucking sweet, Mary."

Words failed her as he grabbed her roughly, drawing her close to him. She didn't fight when he sank a hand into her hair, holding onto the length at the same time as he slammed his lips down on hers.

They were moving as he kissed her. Unable to hold back a moment longer, she pushed the jacket from his arms, then reached around to grip the hair at the base of his neck. Gasping for breath, she cried out as he opened her bedroom door with his back. He didn't stop to close it. Pike broke the kiss long enough to remove her baggy shirt.

She cried out as her hair had been bound with a band, and he tugged on it to release her hair. The slight pain was worth it to have his hands caressing her hair.

"So much fucking better. I love this hair."

Her long brown hair always had a mind of its own, and she struggled to keep it tamed.

His hands moved down from her hair to cup her cheeks. Pike didn't wait around as he slid his hands to her shoulders where the straps of her bra were. Staring into his eyes, she felt his hands move the bra straps down her arms. He caressed around to her back, flicking the catch with ease that showed the practice he had.

She held her hands against the cups to keep her breasts hidden.

"There's no hiding with me, Mary."

He tugged the bra from her hands, and she placed her hands over her breasts. Pike was the first man she'd ever been naked with.

"So beautiful," he said, taking hold of her arms. The pads of his fingers were rougher than she imagined. He eased her hands away as she couldn't fight him. Whatever Pike wanted, he got. She couldn't fight the man she'd been wanting for so long.

This might be her only chance to be with him. For whatever reason, he was taking things to the next level.

His hands moved down to her hips, sliding the sweatpants to the floor. She stood before him naked while he wore everything except for his leather cut that she'd already removed for him.

She waited as he tugged the shirt from his body to reveal his inked covered chest. The Trojan MC insignia covered his chest right over his heart. The horse sign matched the one on his jacket. She'd seen it enough times and had watched Holly doodle the insignia when she was bored.

It wasn't the only ink he had on his body. On his arms were tribal tattoos, the black ink glaring at her over his large muscles. There was not a single speck of color on him. All of his ink was black.

Crossing her legs, Mary followed his hands as they tugged on the belt of his jeans.

"I'm not going to go easy on you, Mary. You've been looking at me for years with those eyes that have begged me to break the rules. I can't wait another moment."

All of her troubles fell away as Pike became her everything. He made her forget about Mac's advances at the diner or her father coming around asking for money. She hated when her parents remembered they had a daughter. No one but Holly had cared for her. For a few moments she wanted to believe that Pike actually cared about her.

He slid the zipper down and kicked out of his boots.

"Eyes to me," he said, when he stood before her naked. The length of his cock was rock hard and stood out in front of him. She couldn't look away as he was so large.

Mary was a virgin, but she'd seen a lot of porn, her intrigue having her searching the 'net for the answers to her questions. She couldn't bring herself to talk to Holly about it, even though her friend had sex. Pike was not lacking in the dick department. In fact, with the size of him, he could have his own porn company and play the lead.

Pushing thoughts of porn and sex aside, she returned her gaze to his.

Pike didn't say anything as he reached out, sinking his hands into her hair and tugging her close. He took control, slamming his lips down on hers. Pike took her hand and wrapped it around his length.

His lips ravished her mouth, taking what he wanted without remorse. She gripped his large arms that dwarfed her and made her feel small in comparison.

He walked her back to the bed, releasing her, and pushing her onto the bed.

"Legs open now," he said.

She spread her legs wide, licking her dry lips as he went to his knees on the floor. He grabbed her legs and dragged her until her pussy was on the edge of the bed.

Mary cried out as he sucked her clit into his mouth, opening the lips of her sex for his searching tongue.

Gripping the edge of the bed, Mary stared up at the ceiling, screaming when her stomach tightened. Pike didn't let up on the assault of her clit. He flicked, sucked, nibbled, and tortured her clit, driving her closer and closer to the edge of orgasm. Unable to contain herself, she started to thrust against his mouth, needing the pleasure to come to an end.

"I'm going to have you so fucking wet. It's going to be easy to slide my cock into your pussy."

He wasn't wrong. His tongue flicked over her clit, and Mary crashed into an earth-shattering climax. Pike wouldn't stop there. Even as she begged and pleaded with him to stop, he wouldn't. He brought her to a second climax within minutes. When her third climax began to build, Pike eased up off his knees, pushing her further up the bed until she lay amongst the pillows.

"Put your feet on the bed and open your legs wide."

She pressed the heels of her feet into the bed, watching him crawl up the bed. His muscles rippled with each crawl he took to get closer to her. She couldn't look away from him and didn't want to.

"Spread the lips of your pussy wide open and don't let go no matter what."

Reaching down, she opened the lips of her pussy so that she was exposed for him to look at. He moved over her with his waist touching her inner thighs.

"Even if it hurts I want you to keep those lips open for my cock."

There were no words as he rubbed the tip of his cock against her clit. Each time he rubbed his dick against her nub, Mary gasped at the sudden explosion of pleasure. She shook with the intensity of it.

"Fuck, you're so wet. You're the best pussy I'm ever going to have. You're better than me, Mary. You'll always be much better than me and you deserve someone better, someone who hasn't killed, but first, I'm going to take what has always been mine."

The tip of his cock moved to her entrance. Her mouth was dry. This was it, the moment she'd wanted for so long.

Pike cupped her cheek, pausing with his shaft at her entrance. They were not joined yet. He stared into her eyes, caressing her skin, and she saw so much emotion flicker across his face.

"Pike?"

Mary screamed as, with one thrust of his pelvis, he slammed deep inside her, tearing through the wall of her virginity. She wanted to move her hands to stop him from thrusting inside her, but his orders stuck in her mind.

The need to please him was there, and she didn't want to look like a failure in his eyes. This shouldn't be happening. Pike held still within her but only for a second.

"Just this once I'm going to have you. I'm going to give you what I've dreamed about." His words were not making sense. Tears filled her eyes at the pain. "I can't have you touch me, otherwise I'll lose myself. It hurts?"

She nodded as words failed her.

"I'll wait until you're ready and then I'm going to give you the ride of a lifetime, you hear me?"

Again, she nodded. What else could she do?

His hands rested on either side of her head, and he took her lips in a tender kiss that didn't match the man she'd come to know. Pike wasn't gentle, at least not that she'd ever seen. He was cruel and demanding. No woman could hold him down, and Mary didn't want to either. She just wanted to matter to someone besides her friend.

"I'm ready," she said. The sting had subsided, and now she wanted to know what it felt like to have him working that giant dick within her. He eased out of her pussy only to slam back inside, going deeper than ever before.

"Your pussy is so fucking tight, Mary. I could spend the rest of my life fucking it." He continued to slam inside her, not giving her the chance to get acquainted with him.

"I-I want to touch you," she said.

"No, no one touches me." She still held the lips of her pussy, and she hated it. The sex, it was amazing and yet something was missing. The pain was still there, only this time the pain was different from the pain in her body.

The orgasm that had started with his tongue subsided. Tears filled her eyes and spilled out of the corners, dripping down either side onto the pillow.

He grunted, closing his eyes. Did it hurt for him to look at her?

"Give me your hands," he said.

She removed her hands from between them, and he locked their fingers together on either side of her head. The only sound in the room was that of their slapping bodies. There was no emotion or moans of pleasure, just an endless sound of smacking flesh.

Why was he doing this?

"Fuck," he said, growling out the word. In the next instance, his cock grew unbearably hard inside her. He'd not worn a condom as the flood of his semen spilled within her.

When it was over, he collapsed over her, and Mary stared at the ceiling, wishing she'd told him no. What had started out amazing had soon turned into something disgusting. Her virginity was gone.

She didn't fight as he pulled out of her, moving to the edge of the bed.

"Now, you can stop thinking about what it would be like to be with me." He got to his feet, but she couldn't bring herself to look at him. Closing her legs, Mary wished he'd just disappear. "You've not got what it takes to please a man like me. I fuck a lot of women, and a virgin pussy is not going to keep me locked up in marriage. I'd cheat, Mary, and hurt you. Find someone else, but at least I got what I wanted."

Mary gasped as she realized he'd gotten what he wanted.

"What was it?" she asked, forcing the words past her lips. She knew, deep down she knew, but she had to hear the words. Pike needed to shatter what little feeling she had left for him.

"I always wanted to claim a cherry for my own."

With those words echoing around the room, Pike left. She heard him grab his jacket seconds later the sound of the apartment door opening and closing. Her heart smashed into a million pieces, and she knew she wouldn't be the same again.

Chapter One

"Are you sure you're all right?" Holly asked, plumping pillows around Mary as she started to walk. Matthew, Duke's son, was standing in the doorway laughing his ass off.

"Don't start or I'm so going to whoop your ass on the court. Use this time to get some practice in," Mary said. She hated this. Ever since she'd left home at eighteen she'd been living with her best friend Holly, but that was back at their apartment, not like this.

"You overdid it at the wedding and now you have to rest. You should have told us the Doctor ordered you to rest."

"It's in a cast, Hols. I wasn't going to miss your wedding day. You'd have picked another bridesmaid, and I wasn't going to let that happen." Mary pushed aside some of her brown hair that had fallen over her eyes.

"She's right," Duke said, walking in. He held a spoon in one hand and a peanut butter jar with the other. "I wasn't waiting around to marry you."

"You're a pain in the ass, both of you," Holly said. "You're on bed rest until that leg comes out of a cast, and I'm coming with you to all of your appointments. I don't trust you, and it's all your fault."

Mary stuck her tongue out at her lifetime friend, at which Matthew laughed and Duke snorted.

"You just stuck your tongue out!" Holly glared at her. "I'll get you back for that, little miss independent."

She couldn't take care of herself, and she'd torn several stitches in her leg for not listening to her doctor. Even though Pike, the bastard that he was, had been the best man, she couldn't bring herself to miss her best friend's wedding.

"I'm sorry. I'm not used to this." She pointed at her useless leg propped up on the coffee table in the luxury of Duke's ranch house. The place was a dream home, designed and built by the man himself. "I like working."

"Mac's holding you a job. Pike saw to that," Duke said, taking a seat beside her on the couch. He offered her a peanut butter laden spoon, and she shook her head.

"I don't want Pike doing any favors for me. I don't need him or want him helping me out."

"You're Holly's best friend. She's my old lady, and what makes her unhappy means I don't get any."

"Dad, ew, I don't need to hear this." Matthew walked away sticking his fingers in his ears.

"If I'm not getting any, the club has a problem. You're club property, Mary. I don't give a fuck if you like it or not. It's the truth."

"I'm sorry." She hated being a lump to everyone. Her parents were a waste of time and did nothing in their life apart from get drunk, screw around, and beat the shit out of their daughter when they could. "I'll make it up to both of you."

"Make us a couple of pies when you're all better and we'll call it even." Duke slapped her thigh, handing her the peanut butter. "I've got to head out to the club." He walked toward Holly. "You good to get Matthew to school?"

"Of course."

Mary couldn't look away as Duke sank his fingers into Holly's long, blonde hair. The love he had for her friend was so beautiful that it made Mary's chest hurt. She'd never get anything like that or even know what it was like to be desired.

Forcing herself to look away, she tried to swallow past the lump in her throat, pushing the tears away.

"I love you," Holly said.

"Love you, too." Duke headed out the door, and Matthew came back into the room carrying a backpack.

"We ready to go?"

"Yep, my dad is picking us up. I really need to learn how to drive." The sound of a horn honking alerted them to Holly's dad, Russ. "Go on out and I'll just finish getting Mary settled."

Matthew didn't argue as he left them alone. "He's a good kid," Mary said.

"Yeah, one of the best and he's doing great at school, so I can't complain."

Chuckling, Mary saw the life her friend had already built up. Holly was Duke's old lady, the stepmother of his son. She had a life, a future.

"I'm so happy for you." Mary smiled at her friend, meaning every single word she said.

"You're going to find that special man for you."

"I'm not. There's no one out there for me." Mary reached up to take hold of her friend's hand. "And that's okay. You know, it's all okay, and I'm not worried about it. Maybe I'll get a cat to keep me going. I think a cat would be nice. The apartment will be a little lonely."

"I've got to talk to Duke about it, but I was thinking of offering you a place to stay here."

"No, Hols. You're a married woman. I will not move in with you. I'm here until the leg gets better. Not a moment longer. I've got plans." She kissed Holly's hand. "Now, go, take your son to high school and then go watch those kiddies."

"Stepmom. I have to be the youngest stepmom to a teenager." Holly laughed. "See you soon."

"Not before I see you first." She picked up the remote on the sofa and flicked on the television. "I hate morning shows." She groaned as a talk show came on.

Groaning, she started to change the channels, wishing she'd brought a couple of cookbooks with her. With a cookbook she'd be set for the day. She loved looking through cookery books to change a recipe to suit her taste. Flicking through the channels, she settled on the cookery channel. She needed a book to jot down notes and ideas. "No one is here to find me."

Putting her leg on the floor, she grabbed her crutches and started moving around the sitting room. When she didn't find a single pad of paper, she moved into the kitchen. Holly would never be in the kitchen without a notepad. Looking from one drawer to another, she cried out in victory when she saw she was right. There was a small notepad that was already stained with grease. In her excitement she'd dropped one of the crutches, and when she turned, her foot banged against the cupboard. Pain flooded Mary, and she lost her grip, dropping in a heap onto the floor.

"Bad move, Mary, very bad move." She went to her elbows, groaning at the position she was in. Tucking the notebook, uncomfortably, into her bra, she grabbed her crutches and started to slide across the floor. "This is so totally humiliating, and now I'm talking to myself. I blame you, Holly."

"Mary?"

As if her day couldn't get any worse. She heard Pike close the front door. Why was he here? Why was he letting himself into Duke's home? Closing her eyes, she rubbed at her temples wishing the ground would just swallow her up so she wouldn't have to face him. Leaning against the cupboard she squeezed her eyes shut trying to catapult herself into another world. This wasn't a movie, though. It was real life, and she couldn't force the world away.

"What are you doing in here?"

Opening her eyes, she stared at the man who had torn her heart out. Pike, the VP to Duke. The club ran through his veins just like his blood. He was a total bastard, and she despised him.

"I'm having a party." The sarcasm dripped from her voice.

"Mary!"

"I was getting a notebook. Why is it so damn important?" Reaching up she started to haul her body off the floor. She was going on a diet and cutting him completely out of her life. She'd lost over ten pounds since that night he'd taken her virginity and cut out her heart. Holly didn't know about Mary's latest promise to herself to diet and get in shape. She'd also joined a gym that she took the bus to get three times a week. With Holly no longer with her, she'd have to find another way to work out.

The whole change to her life was to expel the bad shit, namely Pike. Her life was going to change, and she was determined to move on.

He grabbed her around the waist helping her up.

"Get your hands off me." She struggled against him even as his large hands gripped her waist tightly.

Think about those hands on other women, fucking them, giving them pleasure and not you.

"I'm just trying to help you."

Gripping the counter in front of her, she glared back at him. With one hand still on her waist, he leaned down for her crutches.

Before she could protest, he placed her arm around his neck, and started leading her back to the couch.

"You shouldn't be on your feet."

"How did you know?" she asked, lifting her foot back up to the coffee table. She was tempted to grab her pain pills but decided against them while he was in the room. The pills would only show weakness, and she wasn't weak. She was strong, stronger than ever before.

"I heard Duke telling Raoul about coming and checking on you. Holly's worried."

"Then why are you here?" Reaching into her shirt, she grabbed the notebook and saw she had dropped the pen.

"Here you go." Pike held a pen in front of her.

She took it, thanking him at the same time.

"I decided to come and see how you were doing."

Tapping the pen onto the book she stared at her foot. If she could, she'd walk away from him.

"I always wanted to claim a cherry for my own."

"I'm fine, and you can leave." She opened the book, grabbing the remote to turn the television up. Mary kept herself facing the screen even as Pike moved close to her.

"Mary?"

"Next time tell Duke not to bother to send me anyone. I'm a big girl, and I can take care of myself. I'm here because Holly can't handle me being alone. When I get the all clear from the doctor, I'll be gone." She gripped the book in her hand tightly. Part of her was tempted to leave Vale Valley behind and never look back. Holly had a family, love, and Mary didn't have to worry about her. Once she was out of town she'd forget about this life and finally move on.

"That's not going to happen."

She flinched as he touched her shoulder.

"Mary?"

"Don't touch me please. Get your hands off me." She lifted her hand up in the air as if to ward off a blow. Pike wouldn't physically hurt her. He wouldn't do anything to hurt her.

"I'd never hurt you."

Tears filled her eyes. Pike had hurt her in ways that would stay with her forever.

"Next time Duke wants one of the men to check on me, make sure it's anyone but you."

His hand tightened on her shoulder, but she still wouldn't turn.

"You've got to give me a chance here, baby."

Opening her eyes, she stared straight ahead feeling every inch of his body pressed against her back.

"I don't have to give you anything. You've taken enough. Please leave."

They were both silent. The only sound to be heard was their heavy breathing.

"Mary?"

"I'm sure your presence is being missed at the club. Leave, Pike. I've got nothing to say to you, and there's nothing here for you."

"Look at me."

"No." Licking her dry lips, she tensed up as he gripped the back of her neck. "Just go."

He was going to fight her, refuse to leave. The tension in his body mounted, and yet, he stood up. "Fine, I'll give you space, but it's not going to change the fact we need to talk."

"We don't need to talk."

She whispered the words settling down on the couch once again.

"Don't move around on your leg, as otherwise you'll make me do something you'll regret."

Unable to help herself, she turned to stare at him. "Yeah, like what?"

"I'll take care of you myself. 'Round the clock care at my own place."

She glared at him, folding her arms over her chest. Mary didn't dare say anything in case he wasn't lying. She didn't want to risk it.

When the door closed behind him, she finally let the tears fall.

****

Pike took out the packet of cigarettes in his pocket, and sparked one up. He was so pissed off, at himself and at Mary. Fuck, he hated seeing her hurt, and it was killing him to know she wasn't really taking care of herself.

When he heard Duke talking to Raoul, he'd been so pissed. Why weren't they coming to him to check on her? Before Duke could say anything to him, he was on his bike heading for the ranch.

Taking a deep draw on the cigarette, Pike stared up at the sky wishing for some kind of fucking answer that he knew wouldn't come. Blowing out a puff of smoke, he finally closed his eyes. She'd hurt herself by going to the fucking wedding dancing, and now she was on bed-rest.

She was driving him crazy, and he didn't like it. He'd fucked her a couple of months back, and at the start there had been real fire. The kind of fire you only ever read about or see between really special people like Duke and Holly. She'd flat out scared the shit out of him with what she made him feel. It was never like that with women. Then something snapped. It changed inside him, and he'd turned her first time into shit.

Putting his smoke to his lips, he marched back to his bike and started pushing it out of the driveway. When he got to the gate he saw Raoul enter, stopping as they were about to cross.

"Shit, man, what are you doing here? Duke's been looking all over for you."

"I've checked on her. You don't need to worry."

"I have. My job until Duke gets over the shit I pulled on Holly, I'm on babysitting duty to make amends. He believes it will strengthen my character a little. I don't see why."

"Why?" Pike asked, not really giving a shit about Raoul. He was one of the youngest members of the Trojans MC, and at times he wasn't the smartest, but he had connections.

"I like Mary. She's fun to be with." Raoul smiled at him. "His kid's also pretty cool."

"You touch Mary and I'll cut your dick off and feed it to my fucking dog." He didn't own a dog, but he'd buy one just to go through with his threat.

He wasn't smiling, and Raoul got the message. "Fuck, man, if you want her why don't you fucking claim her? Mary's wanted you for a hell of a long time. No man is getting between those virginal thighs."

Pike tilted his head to the side, glaring at the little shit. "No one talks about her thighs or getting between them, understood?"

"You're a real buzz-kill, you know that?"

Straddling his bike, Pike fired up the engine. "I'll go and talk to Duke. You stay the fuck away from Mary."

Riding out of the ranch, Pike didn't look back, focusing on the road in front of him. Raoul wasn't a bad guy, and he'd learned his lesson with Holly. Everyone in the club knew they didn't stand a chance with her. She'd wanted Duke for a long time, fought it for even longer as he'd been married to a slut at one time. That very slut was six feet under for putting Matthew's life in danger and almost killing Holly.

The same men who'd hurt Holly had also run down Mary as she tried to help her friend. Yeah, the two friends hadn't had the best of luck in the last couple of months. He'd also not been the best highlight of Mary's life.

Driving toward the diner, he parked up outside behind a red pickup truck. His cell phone was ringing and vibrating like shit in his pocket. Turning off his bike so he could think, he answered the phone.

"What?"

"Where the fuck are you?" Duke asked, growling the words down the line.

"In town. I'm getting something to eat."

"You've been to see Mary, haven't you?"

"Maybe." Climbing off his bike, he nodded to a couple of middle-aged broads who smiled at him. He was the same age as Duke and liked a variety of pussy to his little harem. The club offered them of all legal shapes and sizes from young to a little older. He wasn't that interested in young pussy. Mary was the youngest he'd ever had. The very memory of her tight snatch wrapped around his dick had made it impossible to fuck anyone else.

"Fuck, Pike. I told Holly I'd keep you away from her friend. Shit, I'm the fucking president of this bastard club, and if you can't do as I say, there's going to be a few fucking problems."

"Duke, I had to go and check on her. She's hurt herself, and I needed to make sure she was okay."

"It's not your job. Mary wants nothing to do with you. You upset her, she tells Holly, then I'm the one dealing with your problem. I've left it alone for the most part. What went down between the two of you is fucking private, but you bringing it out like this, you're going to make it my problem."

"Has Mary told Holly about it?" he asked, needing to know if she talked to anyone at all.

"No, nothing. It's all pretty silent right now. I don't like it, Pike. Don't fuck with Mary."

"I'm just making a quick stop. I'm hungry."

Hanging up the phone, he headed toward the diner to see Mac. In his pocket he carried over five thousand to pay the man for Mary's absence. Mary didn't have the first clue what he'd been doing for her over the past three years and even before that. He didn't care about her association with Holly. Pike had taken care of her because it was what he wanted to do. He was the one to have a special talk with her parents when her father hit her. Her parents had learned a hard lesson that day. When she'd graduated school he'd been sitting in the crowd, not watching Holly but her. Mary had no one apart from him who cared. He visited the principal's office regularly to make sure her grades were good to great.

Whenever she needed someone he was there, but she didn't know about anything that he'd done to make her life worthwhile. The job she had at the diner with Mac, it wasn't great, yet it paid for her to live in the apartment, that he'd also lined up for Mary and Holly. He paid Mac who then hired Mary and paid her. When the job first started out, Mac had done it for the money. However, Pike knew something had changed. Mac steered clear of Mary, but he made sure Pike knew that he liked Mary, a lot.

He nodded to several of the townsfolk before making his toward the back of the kitchen. Mac stood at the fryer while also flipping a couple of burgers. It was early morning, yet some of the Vale Valley locals always liked to have a burger in the morning. The bacon was sizzling in the background.

"Hey, Pike," Ron, a small kid with red hair, shouted toward him.

"You all right, kid?"

"Yeah."

Mac looked up when Ron started speaking. "Take over here. I've got to talk. Follow me."

He followed Mac to the small office in the back of the kitchen. Mac closed the door behind him, and Pike looked around the small space that was very neatly ordered.

"Mary do this?"

"Yes. She likes order and believes the problems I was having was because I couldn't find anything. I've got a filing cabinet filled with expenses and shit. A very organized life at her hands."

Mac was a good looking man the moment you got him out of the greasy uniform he wore. He wasn't dirty but well kept. His family had owned the diner for a long time, and so when they stepped down, it was only logical for Mac to step up. If not for his family commitment, Pike was certain he'd be staring at another Trojan now. Mac had everything going for him. He was cold, hardened by life and loss, and he could fight. Pike had seen Mac fight just as well as the rest of them.

"Why are you here?" Mac asked, getting down to business.

"Here is the money I owe you."

"You don't owe me shit, Pike. I can't take that. Not anymore."

"You've been taking this for the last couple of years."

"The last couple of years I've been struggling with everything. The food, the customers, money. My folks made this look so fucking easy. It's not, and I'm not the best damn cook there is." Mac ran a hand down his face.

"That why you entered yourself for the fights?" Pike asked.

Being in Vale Valley limited a lot of people in the kind of work they could do. Trojans made good money in their investments and the illegal runs they did. Duke kept them all clean so nothing bad could come back to them. This deal with the Mexicans, running coke, that was as dangerous as they were willing to go. They all lived within thirty miles of the nearest city, and that was where you could find what you need to earn a bit of extra cash, whoring, fighting, and all kinds of weird shit.

"I entered the fights for the money. This place, it wasn't doing good and only barely staying afloat with my folks. I took over, it did worse."

"Mary's helped you, hasn't she? She knows what she's doing and earning her way in gold."

Mac stared back at Pike. "She stopped the grocer from sending me low end products. She was here one day real early and watched me unload the delivery. Before I knew what was happening she took the order form and started to look over the stock. I was paying top money for food that was at its end, which was why I was having to order as often as I was. I was throwing shit out that was rotten. She took over, made sure I got the deal I paid for."

"It's not just that though. She cooks as well. I've seen the improvement in the menu. You're using her."

"I'm paying for her. I couldn't afford her, and yeah, if not for you or Mary's help this place would have been shut down a long time ago. I stopped fighting as we're running at a profit. I don't need your money, and I'm not going to do it to Mary anymore. She deserves better."

Pike stared down at the envelope. "You're taking this money."

Mac shook his head. "I'm not. I've kept my end of the bargain. Mary doesn't know why I first hired her and I'll never tell her. I'll never tell her about your involvement. Everything has changed now."

"You must be losing money with her gone."

"I'm paying her a salary still. Mary, she's an asset to this diner. I'm not going to see my best asset go under just because her boss was an evil bastard who wanted her working."

Pike gritted his teeth. "She's off limits. You don't get to fucking touch her."

"Mary won't let me anywhere near her. I would if she'd let me, but she's got those walls all up. I've not got a chance with her," Mac said. "When we first started out with this, I didn't want anything to do with her. Over the last couple of years, I've come to like her, Pike. This isn't just about you anymore. I care about her."

Pike noticed that Mac didn't say that he hadn't tried to get with her.

"You're not taking the money?"

"No."

Pike didn't want the money. This was the one thing he could give Mary without causing her further pain. Taking her virginity had been the biggest highlight of his life and yet the biggest mistake as well. Throwing the envelope onto the table, he left the office without a backward glance.

Chapter Two

Mary growled with frustration as Raoul helped her toward the toilet. "What did you do to be on babysitting duty?" she asked.

The biker chuckled. "I fucked your friend."

"Yeah, when my leg gets better I'm going to kick your ass again." After Holly had broken down in a fit of tears, Mary had not been able to handle it. She'd found Raoul working on his bike outside of the apartment block where he lived. With no one around she'd literally kicked him up the ass and then grabbed a baseball bat to smack his bike. At the time she hadn't thought much about his lack of retaliation, whereas now she saw he had to have been a good guy. Most guys would have hurt her because she hurt their bike.

"You can kick my ass, but you can't hurt my bike. She's got feelings, too."

She held a crutch under one arm, and her other arm was wrapped around his neck as they hobbled toward the bathroom.

"I'm sick of this shit." Raoul pushed the crutch away and picked her up.

"Are you fucking crazy? I'm huge. You're going to hurt yourself."

"I've carried dead men who've weighed more than you." He walked down the long corridor toward the back of the house. When they were close Raoul kicked the door. "Ah, the toilet awaits." He placed her on her feet. "Do you think you can do everything yourself?"

"I can use the bathroom all on my own. I don't need a babysitter."

Laughing he closed the door, but she didn't hear his footsteps.

"You're standing outside, right?"

"Yep. Boss's orders, baby. I'm to take care of you until you're well. If his woman's not happy, he's not happy, and if he's not happy, then we're all fucked."

She chuckled while pushing her sweatpants down. The clothing she wore was gross, but with the cast, it worked. If she'd listened to the doctor's orders she wouldn't be in this position. She'd have missed Holly's wedding, but she would have been taking a piss without someone waiting outside.

Dropping her head into her hand, she finished her business, flushing the toilet then washing her hands.

Opening the door she saw Raoul leaning against the opposite wall. "Come on, princess." He picked her back up carrying her back to the sitting room. The television was playing to itself.

Letting out a groan, she got comfortable while wishing for something else to do.

"You're bored." He didn't make it a question.

"How did you guess?" she asked.

"Simple. If I was ordered to sit all day I'd lose my fucking mind. What do you need?" he asked.

"A new leg. A new life and to stop being this person." She threw her head back against the couch. "Sorry. I'm not feeling all that positive right now. My leg's in a cast, and I can't do anything. Damn, I so feel like a fourth wheel right now."

"Fourth wheel?"

"Well yeah. You've got Holly, Duke, and Matthew. They're all connected, and there's three of them. I'm fourth, and I'm not part of this little life. I'm not down with this world." She grabbed a pillow to hold close. "I'm feeling sorry for myself right now."

"You're Holly's best friend. The club adores you. You're not anyone's fourth wheel."

"I'm not part of the club. I'm no one's old lady, and I'd never be a club whore." She closed her eyes. "And now I'm talking to the guy who hurt my best friend." She turned her head to look at him. "What you did was seriously uncool."

"I know. It wasn't exactly a moment I was going to sit here bragging about."

"You did at the club."

"I got my ass kicked for it. The guys they're not the same. It was a mistake, and I knew it the moment it happened. I lashed out and hurt Holly in the process."

"If I had a gun I'd shoot you in the dick." She glared at him.

"No, you wouldn't." He moved to sit beside her. "Apart from kicking me up the ass and damaging my bike, you've not got it into you to do any lasting damage. You're too sweet to do anything more."

"You think kicking you up the ass is sweet?"

"It could have been worse."

"How?"

"You could have taken out my dick."

Mary chuckled. "I see what you mean."

She thought about Pike. If she told Holly it would get back to Duke, and in some way, Pike would be forced to pay for what he did. Even Russ, Holly's father, would do something, but it was all because of their love for Holly. Instead, she kept everything to herself. No one but she and Pike knew what happened. "Yeah, I'm too sweet."

"So, what do you want me to do?"

"I don't suppose you'd go to my apartment and get some cookbooks?" She reached down toward her back grabbing a set of keys. "I really am going stir-crazy, but those books should hold it off for a little while."

He took the keys from her. "Stay put, and if I come back to see you on your feet I'm spanking your ass. I don't care what Duke will say. Your ass will be fucking red."

She watched him leaving the room. He was an okay guy.

Folding her arms underneath her chest, she stared at the screen. The whole situation was not inspiring.

"I hate this. I hate being alone."

Most of her life she'd been alone. Her family didn't want anything to do with her. The only person she really had was Holly. "And here we go with the tears. I can't even get a break with those."

She was also talking to herself again, not a good sign.

Lying down on the sofa she stared up at the ceiling. Providing she rested her leg, kept with the exercises that Holly gave her, within a month her cast should be coming off. The doctor was taking an extra precaution because of her going against medical advice.

Lying on the sofa she couldn't help but think about Pike. The way his hands touched her body, gliding through her pussy like he owned it. He *had* owned her body, but he no longer did. She was cutting him out of her life.

In fact she was cutting everyone and everything out of her life. It was time to move on, and the only way for that to happen was to take her life by the balls and to start living.

****

"When I give you a fucking instruction you listen to it, do you understand?" Duke asked, yelling the words across the room. It was rare for Duke to lose his temper, but he was losing it now.

"I understand," Pike said.

"No, you don't understand. You hurt Mary, and if you continue to do so you're going to hurt my wife. She can't be upset right now." Duke gripped the back of the chair, glaring at him.

"Holly can kick me—"

"She's pregnant, Pike. Holly's carrying my kid."

Pike stopped to stare at his best friend. "She's pregnant?"

"I can't have her being upset, and you hurting her friend will upset her."

"Shit, man, congratulations. Did I miss the announcement or something?"

"It's her first kid, and we're keeping it quiet so there are no complications. She doesn't want anyone to know."

"Does Mary know?"

"No. Do you think if Mary knew she'd be at my house now? Mary would find a reason to fucking leave. I'm not going to put Holly through that stress. Those women are like sisters more than friends." Duke turned to look out of the window overlooking the club compound. "What happened, Pike?"

"I did what I had to do."

He wasn't going to tell anyone about what happened. It was between him and Mary.

"You know when I caught Julie fucking around on me I didn't give a shit. Good riddance. I had all the pussy I could ever want, and I fucked it. The club, it was everything to me even with Julie hanging around. She didn't bother me. I only married her because she was pregnant."

"What are you trying to get at?" Pike asked.

"None of the pussy mattered to me. Yeah, it was good enough to fuck but not to take home to my kid. Holly, she has been on my radar for fucking years, but you know me, no illegal pussy. The shit with Raoul, I couldn't claim her them. Now, she's mine. I've got a ring on her finger. She's in my house, in my bed, with my kid inside her. I'm not going to hurt her."

"You've been very lucky."

"Once you find the woman for you, Pike, it doesn't matter how much pussy is lying around begging you to fuck it. Nothing is going to mean as much to you as sinking into the pussy that you call your own." Duke nodded at him, rounding his desk. "You can leave."

Pike didn't see a reason to prolong talking and left the office.

Glancing around the room he saw Daisy sat at the bar nursing a coffee. Chip, Pie, Smash, and Knuckles were playing cards. The other boys were playing a game of pool.

Sitting beside Daisy, he saw the big guy rubbing at his temples.

"Good night?"

"Shit, Pike, keep it quiet. I've got a fucking army of hammers in my skull."

Chuckling he looked across the bar to see Baby staring back at him. Baby was a beautiful little blonde with a tight pussy and suction on her mouth that men dreamed about. She'd been voted in as a club whore three months ago. The men loved her, but Pike hadn't tried her out yet. Since being inside Mary he'd not been with another woman. He'd tried, boy, had he tried, but he just couldn't.

Pike had taken several women up to his room in the hope of moving on like he'd told Mary. Nothing. The women, they were pros and couldn't get him to get it up. They'd sucked on his dick, rubbed against him, even given him a little girl on girl show, but nothing. His dick was broken.

Yet when he was in the shower with just his hand and images of Mary, he came like a fucking champion. The bitch, his woman, had broken his dick for anyone else.

"Good party last night?"

"What can I get you, Pike?" Baby asked. She thrust her chest out, begging for attention.

"Was it a good party last night?" Pike asked, pointing to the coffee machine. He wasn't in the mood to be trashing his bike this early in the day.

"I took care of Daisy last night. Me and Samantha did. That girl has got a tighter pussy than I have," Baby said, handing him a drink.

"You got two lots of pussy?"

"Fuck yeah, I did. I earned it," Daisy said, groaning and gripping his head.

"What about you, Pike? Do you want to taste me?" She leaned over the counter to run her hand down his chest. "I'm better than the guys say. I know exactly what I'm doing and how good to do it."

She pressed her tits together to give him a good view.

Pitiful. His dick was flaccid. No life in it at all.

"Sorry, baby, not today." He pushed her hand away taking a sip of his coffee. His life couldn't get any worse right about now.

Grabbing his drink, he left Baby to pout and Daisy to nurse his hangover. Heading up to his room, he closed and locked the door. Bitches knew not to come into his space. This was where he went to be alone. They were allowed inside his space if they were invited. He kept a clean room as mess had always annoyed him. Putting his coffee on the bedside cabinet, he removed his leather cut to place it inside his wardrobe. His life consisted of the club and nothing else. He owned a small house on the opposite of town. It wasn't large like Duke's but modest, something he never thought he'd have in life. His folks were off living up the good life that they'd gotten through saving every dime they earned. They called in from time to time, but that was rarely. His father had served his time in the Trojans and walked away with his wife.

It was rare for families in the club not to lose something. Russ, the previous president, had lost a child and almost his marriage. Duke had killed the woman who gave birth to Matthew as she'd put the whole club in danger. There were men he called brothers who had each lost something.

Sitting on his bed, he opened the drawer that kept his secrets. Pulling out the single photo of Mary, he smiled. The day he'd taken this shot was the day she graduated. Holly wasn't in the picture, which was a first for the two. Pike had taken full advantage and snapped a shot.

She was a beautiful woman, perfect in every way, but he couldn't bring himself to hurt her. In all of his life he'd never had a woman to call his own, never needed to own a pussy that was exclusively his. He liked variety, and in time he just knew he would hurt Mary. Duke's words came back to haunt him. They wouldn't last, he was sure of it.

Putting the photograph back in the drawer, he slammed shut the past. There was no room in his life for Mary. His life was part of the club, VP to Duke, and fucking pussy when his dick would allow.

Chapter Three

"You really didn't need to come to see me, Mac," Mary said, hobbling around on her crutches. It had been a week since Holly demanded she stay with her. Raoul was in the kitchen making them all a drink as Mary walked around the room, doctor's orders. Her leg was doing fine, but he wanted her to take it easy, start walking but not doing too much.

"I wanted to see you. It's not the same at the diner without you."

"Ah, you need me back to cook. You're overcooking the burgers, right? Giving them well done burgers when they want medium?" She teased. Mac was a good guy. He was fun to be around and easy to talk to when he didn't try to get into her pants. Fortunately he'd stopped trying, which was all right with her.

After what Pike did she wasn't interested in repeating the experience. Hearing Holly and Duke go at it though, listening to them made her yearn for what they had. Matthew had given her a music player with large headphones. The kid was smart, and when the moans started, Mary played her music as loud as she could to drown them out. She'd never heard Holly scream in orgasm before, and she hoped to never hear her again.

"Everyone misses you, and it's not always about the food. You're a well-loved person, Mary." He stood up, taking the crutches from her, and leading her back to the sofa. "Don't overdo it. Not listening to doctor's orders is what got you here."

"I'm dying here. Can't I go out? Doctor didn't say anything about going out? You can take me back to the diner? I'll sit in the back, helping out. I promise I won't be a nuisance."

She couldn't spend another day watching television or playing cards with Raoul. He cheated anyway so that she'd never win.

"Mary?"

"Please, oh please?" she asked, gripping his shirt. "If I don't leave this house I'm going to go insane. How can I help you from a mental hospital, huh?"

"She can go," Raoul said. "I'll stick around the diner."

"What about your leg?" Mac asked.

"You've got your car. I can ride with you."

She smiled up at him, doing her best to look desperate. The weekends weren't so bad as Holly was around with Matthew and they spent time in the yard. The weekdays, they were a complete and total nightmare.

"Fine. Come on." Mac held his keys and helped her toward the car. Raoul followed behind, handing over the crutches.

"I'll follow on my bike after I lock the house up, okay?"

"I won't be going anywhere," Mary said, smiling. It was nice to finally have the wind in her hair and the sun on her face. It was icy cold, as it was January, but she didn't mind. Being outside was fun.

"The club better not have my ass for this."

"The club doesn't own me, Mac. You know this." She reached over to tap his hand. It was a shame that she didn't have any feelings about Mac. They'd been on dates, but they weren't real, at least to her they weren't. He was nice, a gentleman to her. They shared a lot of the same interests. They both liked to cook and bake. The diner was important to them, and they liked the same movies, books, and got along like best friends.

Mac didn't ring any of her bells. She didn't feel anything for him other than caring about him.

"Pike would make it his business."

"He doesn't get a say in what I do, Mac. Don't bring him up. He's not important." In the last week while she'd been alone when Raoul had to leave she'd started working on her life once the cast came off. She'd decided she wasn't going to leave town, but she'd paid for a full year's gym subscription that started in a month's time. There would no longer be any dawdling in her life about making plans.

"He hurt you, Mary. You've got to talk about it."

"If I was going to talk about it to anyone it would be Holly. You're my boss, and I care about you. Anyway, I was thinking about the diner. I've got some suggestions I'd really like you to consider."

"Of course."

For the next ten minutes on the drive into town, Mary told Mac about her ideas of allowing a themed diner that changed menus throughout the year. For Halloween they could do pumpkin soup and something with candy corn. Christmas would be a festive treat of candy canes and turkey.

"This could make our diner different, unique, and bring the locals in and even some tourists?" Mac pulled up behind the diner. "What do you think?"

"I think you're in the wrong business as a waitress. There's something I wanted to talk to you about." He climbed out of the car and rounded the vehicle to her side. She stared at him as he knelt down beside her. "Mary, how would you feel about becoming a partner in the diner?"

"A partner?"

"Yes, like my mom and dad. They were partners."

All happiness at his suggestion fell away. "Mac, erm, I don't want to hurt your feelings, but I don't want to marry you." She stared at her hands for several seconds before chancing a look at him. He was smiling back.

"I wasn't asking you to marry me, baby. I know you're not ready for something like that. I'm asking as friends. Don't get me wrong. I care about you, but I know that's not going to happen."

"Friend partners?"

"Friend partners." He offered her a hand.

"Deal." She smiled as she shook his hand.

"Okay, let's get you out of here."

"Mac, what's going on?"

Mary froze at the sound of Pike's voice. Why did he have to show up now? He was spoiling her moment. Mac didn't stop helping her out. With her arm wrapped around Mac's neck, they both turned to face the scary-assed biker. She doubted Mac was afraid of Pike. She was. He looked pissed off.

"I'm helping Mary inside."

"Does Holly know she's gone from the house? Where the fuck is Raoul?"

"He's joining us after he's locked up Duke's ranch," Mary said. "What are you doing here, Pike? It's none of your business what I do." She gripped Mac's shoulder tighter. This was not what she wanted to do today with him. She never wanted to get into it with him.

"I don't think so," Pike said. He stepped closer shoving Mac out of the way. Neither of them was expecting the action so Mac stumbled onto his ass and Mary reached out to grip something. Pike caught her around the waist. "You're not going into work, not today. You're a week into your recovery and you want to mess it up."

"The doctor didn't say anything about me being cooped up all day alone."

"Raoul's there."

"You think I like watching television? Is that what you think? Mary's got a fat ass so she must have got it eating too much and sitting on her fat ass all day?" She was losing her temper. His hands on her waist were not helping her any either. "Let go of me."

"Pike!" Mac warned.

"No, this is club business, Mac. Stay the fuck away from her."

Pike lifted her up in his arms, carrying her toward a blue pickup.

"Mary?" Mac said.

"I'll be okay, Mac." She waved a hand at him, knowing when she and Pike were alone, she was going to hurt him. This man had no right to come bombarding into her life and forcing her to do what he wanted.

He placed her in the passenger side of the car, locking the door behind him.

"Asshole!"

Reaching into her sweatpants she grabbed her cell phone. Putting Holly's number ready to dial, she screamed as Pike threw her cell out of the window. The device smashed on impact.

"That was my only fucking phone, you brute." She slapped him hard in the chest, hoping he'd feel some kind of pain.

"You're acting like a spoiled brat."

"And you're acting like an overbearing idiot. Why are you even here?" she asked, folding her arms underneath her chest.

"I followed you. I thought it was strange for Mac not to be at the diner. I shouldn't have been surprised to find him at Duke's place."

"Stay out of it. Mac is a perfect gentleman."

"No, he's not, and you're a fucking idiot for even thinking he is." Pike pulled out of the diner, and they passed Raoul on the way. He didn't stop to talk to the other biker. "You're a fucking pain in my ass."

She stayed silent, not wanting to get into it with him.

"You're supposed to be on rest. How do you think Holly's going to feel when she finds you gone like that?"

Screaming, she turned to glare at him. "This is my life, and you just ruined another fucking moment of it so thank you."

"Another moment?"

"Mac just asked me to be his partner with the diner. I'm going to get a say in the running of the diner. I'm not just going to wait tables anymore. I'll be creating a piece of beauty in Vale Valley, something I've wanted for a long time. I was happy, and you came along and spoiled it."

"That's one moment, and Mac should have given you that months ago. You've helped him out of a rut with your organizing and recipes. He should be paying you twice the salary you're on."

"How do you know I organize his life?" she asked.

"I saw the office, and he told me."

"Mac works for the Trojans?" Mac hadn't told her that. He was friends with the club. Everyone in Vale Valley was friends with them or at least friend of a friend. She didn't know Mac did business with the club.

"He doesn't."

"Then why were you in the office?"

"What other moment did I ruin?" he asked, glaring at her.

She was tempted to ignore him. Her life had been a lot easier when she ignored the problem around her and only focused on what was important in her life. Pike had hurt her and hurt her worse than her parents or any bully.

"You ruined the moment you took my virginity. I'll never get that back or replace that memory. Neither will I replace this moment with Mac in my life. I'm tired of you always being there and ruining everything."

She forced the tears back down. He didn't need to know the power he had to make her cry.

Maybe leaving Vale Valley wasn't such a bad idea.

"You're planning on leaving?"

Oops, she'd spoken aloud.

"You're thinking of leaving town?"

Letting out a sigh, she stretched her neck back wishing for the strength to deal with the man beside her.

I hate him. I hate him. I hate him.

He ruins everything he touches.

I hate him. I hate him. I hate him.

"Yes, I've thought about it. It's time I moved on out of town. There's nothing here holding me down." She gripped the back of her neck, to stretch out the tight muscles.

"You're not leaving town."

"It's none of your business what I do, Pike."

"I'm making it my business."

****

He'd gone to check on her. That was all Pike had done. It had been a week since he'd seen her. Most of the time he'd get his Mary fix by either seeing her through town, with Holly, or at the diner. This week with her locked up at Duke's, he'd not seen her. He couldn't just show up at the house for no reason and then he had to think about Holly. Driving into town, he'd picked up Mary's favorite cream bun from the diner only to discover Mac wasn't even in. There was only one place Mac would go, and he found the bastard with Mary. Fuck, it was all his fault. He'd put the two together without thought. Mac was to keep an eye on Mary while she worked, show her attention but not to touch.

Rubbing at his temples, Pike's anger rose. Everything was fucked up and now he was heading toward the clubhouse. Raoul was a waste of fucking space. No one was keeping Mary safe from herself. Didn't they see how crazy she was getting? Glancing over at her, he saw her gripping the hem of her sweatshirt. Sitting around doing nothing was driving her crazy. She hated not doing anything.

"Why are we going to the clubhouse?" she asked.

"I've got business to deal with."

"Take me back to town or take me home. I don't want to go to the clubhouse."

"Too bad you can't follow orders." He took the steep turn and saw Duke waiting for him outside of the clubhouse. The phone he had to his ear lowered when he caught sight of them.

Turning off the ignition, Pike let out a breath.

"Stay here."

"You've got to be crazy," Mary said, slamming open the car door, playing right into his hands without even knowing it.

"What the fuck is this, Duke? I got a call from Raoul—"

"He kidnapped me," Mary said, using the truck to move forward. She looked damn cute when she was angry.

"What the hell are you doing here, Mary?" Duke asked.

"I went to check on her when I found her leaving your house with Mac. She's not taking her own care into account. She's reckless, Duke," Pike said.

"You're an asshole, Pike. I was spending some time at the diner with Mac. I wasn't going to be doing anything. I'm going crazy in that house."

"Crazy enough to put her own care back. Holly doesn't need to be worrying about Mary during the day." He gave Duke a pointed look.

"What are you trying to do?" Duke asked.

"Raoul's not the man for the job. He's not got what it takes to put this woman in her place."

"In my place, are you completely insane?" Mary asked, having to gain her balance on the hood of the truck. The moment she did, Pike smiled. She realized what she'd done by acting out irrationally. "You bastard."

"She needs someone who'll care about her around the clock. Who's not afraid to make her sit on her ass, even tie her the fuck down. You're busy, Raoul's not the man for the job, and Holly, she's got a lot on her case right now."

"You want to do it?" Duke asked. The moment Holly was mentioned Duke was on board.

"I'll do it."

"Don't you dare. I will tell Holly about this."

"Does she have her cell phone?" Duke asked, looking at her before returning his gaze to Pike.

"Her cell phone died on the pavement."

"Take her to your place. Give me a couple of hours with Holly before you let her call." Duke slapped him on the back. "You better take care of this properly. I will not be having Holly's wellbeing under threat."

"I will, Duke."

He rounded back to Mary, who was glaring at him. "You planned this."

"You're going to find out there's a lot about me that's unexpected."

Raoul drove into the compound as Duke was heading toward his bike. "You can't even keep a woman safe. We're going to have a serious fucking talk when I get back."

Pike grabbed his woman, placing her in the truck. "I hate you," she said.

"I know." He closed the door.

Climbing behind the wheel, he started up the truck again.

"I can't believe you did this."

"All you had to do, Mary, was rest and get better. You couldn't do it, and now it's up to me to deal with you."

"I don't want you to be anywhere near me." Her hands were shaking, and he saw her fist them on her lap.

"I know. We're going to make a pit stop at your house. I'll grab some of your stuff and then we'll go to my place."

"I really hate you right now. You can't just leave everything alone, you've got to interfere. Doesn't it even occur to you that I don't want anything to do with you?" she asked.

"It does, but you see, I don't care."

She growled, folding her arms over her chest to stare out of the window. He didn't mind. She could keep growling and getting angry. It was up to her what she wanted to do. Mary had a right to be angry.

Parking up outside of her apartment, he let himself in going straight to her room. He'd not been back here since that night. Staring at the bed, his cock went from flaccid to rock hard within a matter of seconds. The tightness made it hard for him to move. Fuck, he'd not had a hard-on like this since being inside her. He remembered how tight and wet her little pussy had been, all slick and juicy.

Rubbing his cock, he grunted at the instant shot of pleasure throughout his body. He needed to get his mind on something else, not on the bitch in the car.

She's not a bitch.

He'd call her anything to stop these feelings running through his body.

Opening up a bag, he packed her clothes, not really seeing anything he was picking. When her clothes were packed, he grabbed her underwear, paying a little more attention to what he was putting inside.

Once he was packed, he entered the kitchen, grabbing the few titles that were left. At his own place he'd already bought her a selection of cookbooks for her to browse through.

Closing up the door, he headed toward the truck to see her crying.

Letting out a sigh, he placed the bags in the back of the truck. "Why are you crying?" he asked, climbing back behind the wheel.

"Nothing."

"You've got to open up to me for me to help you."

"I don't want your help."

Starting up the truck, Pike made his way toward his home. None of the club whores had even made it to his place. He fucked them in the club and rarely in his own room.

"Where are we going?" she asked.

"To my place."

"No one goes there." She voiced his earlier thoughts.

"Consider yourself lucky. You're going to be the first one."

"I don't think that's lucky at all," she said.

He didn't say anything. She was still hurting even though she tried to hide it. Glancing across at her, he only got the side of her profile. She refused to even look in his direction. Did she still have feelings for him? Did she ever think about that night?

Gritting his teeth, Pike cursed himself. He was not a fucking pussy-whipped asshole. No woman held him down with her pussy. This was all fucking crazy and insane.

Neither of them spoke for the rest of their journey. When he pulled up outside of his modest home, he held onto the steering wheel tightly.

"I've not got my crutches," she said.

He'd not picked them up for the reason he didn't want her to use them. She needed to be completely dependent on him. "I'm taking care of you."

Turning off the ignition, he took her bags inside the house before going back for her. Her door was open, and the cold was making her nipples rock hard pebbles. Reaching up, he took her into his arms. She was tense, and he pushed the door closed.

"You've got absolutely no care about your own personal safety, do you?"

"I don't know what you mean." She held him as loosely as she could. He was tempted to pretend to drop her just to feel her clawing at him. Pike held her close.

Kicking the front door closed, he moved to the sitting room, placing her on the sofa.

"Now, you're going to stay there and keep that leg rested."

"What happens if I make a run for it, officer?" she asked. Her eyes were hard points, glaring back at him. Her temper was only making him hotter than hell for her. He'd give anything to push her over the edge of the couch, drop her sweatpants, and slide his dick into her hot little cunt.

"I'll turn you over my knee and spank your ass. You're in my house now, under my rules. Disobey them and there will be punishment, Mary."

"You can't keep me here. Don't you have a whole harem of women to keep you satisfied?"

"They can do without me for a couple of days."

"You're a pig."

"And I'm going to get your room set up." He left her alone, handing her the remote. "You throw it at me and I won't bring it back to you." He gave her a warning. Mary had been coddled too damn much. It was time for her to meet a brick wall.

He took her bags down to his room. There was a spare bedroom that would put a lot of space between them, but he didn't want her there. He liked the idea of her being next to him.

The channels were being changed repeatedly as she went up and down. Sitting on the edge of his bed, Pike stared ahead at his reflection. For the first time in his life he looked nervous.

"Once you find the woman for you, Pike, it doesn't matter how much pussy is lying around begging you to fuck it. Nothing is going to mean as much to you as sinking into the pussy that you call your own."

Mary's pussy was his. No other man had known how good she was nor did they know anything about her. He'd made it his business to know everything about her. One stupid mistake, one stupid thought, and he'd hurt Mary in ways he'd tried to avoid.

You know what you want. What you crave.

Getting to his feet, he walked back into his sitting room. Mary sat with the remote pointed at the screen looking totally miserable. This was the woman he'd wanted, and he screwed it up, betrayed her trust, and in turn betrayed himself.

"Come on, Mary. It's time for us to make a change," he said, entering the room. He took the remote from her.

"What do you think you're doing?" she asked. He picked her up, carrying her down to the bathroom.

"You're in the worst pair of sweatpants I've ever seen. It's time for you to be more yourself."

"What?"

"You're getting a shower."

****

"All I asked was for Mary to stay in our house and now you're telling me she's gone with Pike?" Holly asked. Her arms were flying about all over the place. Raoul winced as her voice got even louder, grating on his nerves.

Raoul sat in Duke's office. The man himself was behind the desk watching his wife. The love and lust was easy to see.

"Pike's going to take care of her. Neither you nor I could have stopped him, Hols. You know that."

"Mary can't stand him. She's going to think I betrayed her."

"You didn't. You're working. I can't be there to babysit her. Raoul's no good at looking after her."

"I did my best. She was doing fine until Mac came to see her. She wanted to get out and do shit," Raoul said. He'd fucked up with Holly, but he'd not fucked up on anything else in the club.

"You can go," Duke said, glaring at him.

"Look, I know you don't like me for what I did to her, and I accept that. It doesn't mean you can keep treating me like shit. I earned my patch into the club.

Take them away if I lose the right to call myself a Trojan." He stormed out of the club, angry and pissed off.

Gripping the back of his head, he yelled. Leaving the clubhouse he saw Daisy cleaning his bike with Baby sitting on the wall beside him. She wore a small skirt, smaller than Raoul had ever seen it. He'd been part of bringing her into the club, fucking her while the rest of his brothers watched. She had a nice tight pussy. With all the dick she was getting lately, he doubted it would be nice and tight for very long.

"I need to get out of here. You want to come to the city for a while?" Raoul asked.

"Sure."

"Oh, can I come?" Baby asked.

"No, brothers only." Raoul wanted to get some pussy that didn't belong to the club. For that he couldn't have any club whores hanging around his neck.

"You heard the man, Baby. You're going to have to find another man for the night."

Baby pouted but walked away to leave them alone.

"Are you okay, man?"

"No. I'm going to enjoy what life I've got left before Duke decides to take it away." Raoul straddled his bike.

"He's not going to kill you."

"No, he's going to do something much worse."

"Oh, yeah, like what?"

"Vote me out of the club."

Chapter Four

"You're not taking me for a shower. Pike, I mean it. Let go of me."

"You're miserable, depressed, and in a fucking pissy mood. You're having a wash, and then we're going to put you in something that wouldn't fit a small elephant." He tugged on her sweatshirt. "Who bought you these? They're horrible."

"I did."

"They're easily four sizes too big."

"No, they're fine." She wanted to fight him, but if he released her she could end up on her ass all embarrassed. "I seriously hate you right now."

"I thought you hated me before."

"I did. Now it's worse. Besides, I can't go in the shower. I've got my cast."

"That's okay. I can wash you myself."

"You're not coming anywhere near me," she said.

He pushed open a door that revealed a large bed. Pike didn't stop there. He went straight through to a large bathroom. Pike placed her on the toilet seat near a large sink.

"If you even try to leave I will tie you to my fucking bed and wash you while you can't move."

"This is a form of abuse. I'm sure it is."

"And what you're doing to yourself, that's a form of abuse. You've got to learn to take care of yourself."

"I've been doing it all my life. I know how to take care of myself."

"No, you know how to survive. There's a big fucking difference." He placed several towels around the toilet and filled the large sink with water. She watched as he grabbed a sponge and a bar of soap. "What do you think?" He placed the soap in front of her to sniff.

The vanilla scent was nice.

"Yes, I like it."

He placed the soap into the water before he faced her. "You're going to get naked, Mary, if you like it or not."

"I don't want to get naked." She folded her arms over her breasts.

"I've seen it all before."

"I know. It didn't make much impression, remember?"

His jaw clenched. "I'm trying to take care of you."

She lifted her head up to the ceiling, wishing for anything to happen but this.

"Mary, I'm going to wash your body."

"I didn't expect anything else. You need to understand, Pike, when it comes to you, I don't expect anything from you." She tightened her hands at the hem of her shirt.

It's just a shirt and a wash.

She'd refused Holly's help and Raoul's when he offered. Cleaning herself had been difficult, and she'd really like to feel clean.

Pulling her shirt from her body, she placed it on her lap. Pike tugged it out of her hands, throwing the shirt in the trash.

"Hey, that's my shirt."

"It's a horrible shirt. Trust me, the trash bin is being nice to it."

"Why are you doing this?" she asked, crossing her arms over her chest. He was right though. The clothes she wore were the least attractive and horrible.

"Taking care of you?" She nodded. "Because I've been doing it for a lot longer than you realize. Get your bra off."

"I'm not going to sit here naked in front of you."

"I've seen it all before."

"And I don't want you to see it again." She fumed inside. This was not going with her plan of ignoring him. It was too damn hard to ignore the man right in front of her when he looked as hot as he did.

Ignore the emotions. He doesn't care about me.

"You don't think I see you naked? I see you all the time, Mary. When I close my eyes I know how damn fucking full your tits are. I know what it's like to suck them in my mouth and to give you unbelievable pleasure. No one is ever going to take away the taste of your cunt or what it was like to slide into your tight pussy, but it doesn't mean I don't imagine taking you again."

She was in shock. There was no way she was going to fall for his shit or risk getting her heart broken.

Taking off the bra, she crossed her arms over her chest, staring directly at his chest so she didn't have to look into his eyes. He knelt in front of her. His large hands going to her waist to slowly drag her sweatpants down. He couldn't go anywhere with her sitting on them.

"You're going to have to release those tits of yours, baby."

"Don't call me, baby."

Come on, Mary, you can do this. He doesn't mean anything to you. Just lift your ass up and treat him like this doesn't matter.

She found a part of herself that she thought had died the night he broke her heart. The part of her that fought against her feelings for Pike and allowed her to get on with her life. She hadn't sat around waiting for Pike to come to his senses and see her. No, she'd lived her life, had fun, and at times completely forgotten Pike existed. Okay, that last one was a little extreme, but it had happened. She didn't need to care that he saw her naked.

He'd seen a lot of women naked. There was nothing special about her.

Lowering her arms she stared down at Pike without any thought.

"That's my girl."

She didn't respond.

Lifting herself off the seat he dragged down her sweatpants. She wasn't wearing any panties, so she didn't have to worry about that.

Placing her hands in her lap, she watched him get to his feet. He reached into the cabinet over the sink pulling out two grips. When he returned she didn't fight him as he gathered her hair up and placed the grips inside.

"We'll do your hair soon," he said.

She sat still, trying to talk her body into not reacting to what he was doing. It was damned difficult as his fingers glided across her skin. There was something intimate about him taking care of her. Pike didn't rush, nor was he rough with her. Instead, he took his time, washing her body. He'd lather soap over her skin then use the sponge to wipe it away. When he used the soap, he touched her the most. His fingers and palms were sliding all over her body.

Mary didn't have a choice but to close her eyes as he washed over her chest. She'd not had any touch to her breasts since him. God, she needed to get more experience in before she lost her mind with ghost memories of him. He'd not even been that great. Their time together had started out hotter than anything she'd ever read before. Halfway through, it had fizzled out, and become nothing.

Shaking her head, she chuckled.

"What are you laughing at?" he asked.

"Nothing, really."

He was using a towel to dry her body. Her cheeks had to be bright red from when he washed her pussy.

"I'll be happy to hear it."

Letting out a sigh, she glanced over at him. "Really?"

"Yeah."

"Okay, I was thinking about the time we … fucked." Lifting her hand in the air, gesturing between them, Mary started to ramble. "Well, I was thinking how hot it started out. I mean it was off the charts, at least for me it was. I don't know what happened, but it sort of died in the middle and grew lame by the end. Kind of boring, nothing like the earth-shattering sex I've read about. But then, stories lie, don't they?"

She tilted her head to the side to smile at him.

The grip he held on the sponge would have killed a human if he could get his hands on them. Mary was thankful it was just a sponge.

"You did it on purpose, didn't you?" she said, getting it. Holly and Duke screwing at their home, there was no dying lust in the middle. Holly cried out, begging for more up until the final peak.

Pike didn't say anything.

"Wow, you took my cherry, which is what you wanted, and you couldn't even give me a good time." She shook her head at his selfishness. "You know what, you're right. I'm done. I'm totally done with all of this. I'll be here for you to take care of me, but you don't have to worry about me at all, Pike. Seriously, I'm totally over you. I won't act like Holly did with Raoul. I'll still come to the clubhouse with her. I won't make your time uncomfortable. I'm done."

She gripped her thighs, begging herself not to let the tears fall. He'd not even made it a memorable first experience in a good way. No, Pike only gave her the worst of memories.

Mary wasn't lying. She was done caring about him and what he did.

****

Once Pike finished cleaning her, he washed the bathroom putting away the soap and sponge that he used. Glancing at Mary, he couldn't help the arousal flooding to his cock. She looked so beautiful as she tapped her fingers on the counter near the sink. Mary wasn't even trying to cover up her body. In fact it was like she wasn't even naked as he looked at her.

Her tits were exactly like he remembered them, large and full. The red tips of her nipples were calling for him to suck, lick, bite.

He placed a towel around her, leading her back toward the kitchen.

"I'm naked."

"I know."

Placing her on the chair, he moved toward the fridge. He had already fully stocked his home with everything he'd need to take care of her. Glancing toward her, he saw she was checking out the kitchen. Smiling, he set to work on making them both sandwiches. He couldn't cook, never enjoyed it, never wanted to, yet his kitchen was filled with all of the top of the range equipment. Neither Mary nor Holly knew that he'd broken into their apartment to find what Mary would need. He saw Mary kept a wish list of items she always wanted along with a catalogue.

Pike had spent the morning at their place writing out every item and design that she'd scribbled over. When he got home, he'd ordered everything.

"This is nice," she said.

"Thanks."

Buttering slices of bread, he placed a square of cheese on each sandwich before adding a slice of ham followed by a pickle. This was the food he lived on when he was alone.

He placed the finished sandwich in front of her, liking her naked in his space.

She picked up the food without complaint, biting into it.

Pike watched her eat. The way her plump lips went around the sandwich, biting down. His cock thickened as he imagined those lips on his cock, taking him deep. She wouldn't know the first thing about sucking a man's cock, but he could teach her. There was a lot he could teach her.

There were a few crumbs at the side of her mouth. She brushed them away before he got a chance to touch her.

"You know what, you're right. I'm done. I'm totally done with all of this."

Her words echoed around his mind making his gut clench. He didn't want her to be done with him. The thought of losing her made his chest hurt. Mary had been his for so long that the thought of not having her gaze following him around made him sick to his stomach.

"You don't cook."

"I know."

Tilting his head to the side, he looked at her.

"Everything here, it's like a dream." She smiled, taking the second sandwich and biting into it.

"Yeah, I was thinking if you're a good girl and get well then this could be your reward."

"What?" Her gaze landed on him.

"I'll never use this kitchen, but it's all fully stocked." He got out of his chair and started walking around the room, opening cupboards to show her how well stocked everything was. "I'm not going to use it." Going to her side, he wrapped an arm around her waist, helping her up. "And I know you will. Between you and Holly, this could work for you better than that apartment." He moved to the door and opened it, switching on the light. Pike had installed a large pantry fit to serve royalty. None of the brothers knew he'd spent his time researching everything Mary would need, flours, sugars, baking powders and sodas, chocolate, all kinds. Everything was there for the baker and cook.

"Why would I use this? I've got a kitchen of my own."

"Not like this. Your kitchen is so small. I wouldn't mind you working here, testing out your recipes."

"What do you get out of this?" she asked.

"I get to see you get well and I get to taste everything you've made." *And I don't have to worry about Mac giving you better.*

"This is, wow, it's amazing."

"No conditions either. All you've got to do is get better." While she was getting better he'd make sure her apartment was emptied and then he'd spring other things on her as well. All in good time. Pike didn't expect this to be an overnight success, just the start. He'd hurt her too damned bad to expect her to forgive him instantly. It had taken him a long time to come to the conclusion that he couldn't live without her. Pike was going to make her his. "What do you say?"

"I say yes. A fool would turn down this opportunity, and I can promise you, Pike, I'm no fool."

She shook in his arms, going giddy.

He laughed along with her.

"This is like Christmas has come all at once. Sorry, I'm a little excited."

He chuckled, pleased to have finally done something to make her smile. There were times when they were growing up where he had made her smile.

"I don't suppose you'll help me wash your hair now?" he asked. The long brown length was shiny with grease, and it wasn't a good shine either. He wanted her to be happy.

"Yes. Please, I can't stand the way my hair feels." She scrunched up her nose looking adorable.

Come on, Pike, you can do this.

He didn't know what he was doing. When he'd taken her virginity a couple of months back, he'd intended to walk away without looking back. He figured he'd move onto several different kinds of pussy. The Trojans MC clubhouse was full of willing, available pussy, and yet he'd not had one. The only satisfaction he'd gotten in the last few months was from his own hand. Duke was right. The moment you found a pussy for yourself, there was no turning back. No man had known the pleasure of being inside Mary. She was all of his, not Mac's, not Raoul's, his.

Baby, the club whore, didn't appeal to him. The only woman who got him hard was the woman in his arms now. Even with her ratty looking hair she made him hotter than hell. She was biting her lip as they walked back toward the bathroom. He wanted to suck that lip into his mouth.

He set her back on the toilet before returning to his office. The large computer chair would work a lot better to get her at the sink. She sat in the same spot where he left her. Easing her into the chair, he placed it in front of the sink.

"This?" he asked, holding some shampoo up for her to see.

"Yes."

Pike moved the chair, leaning her back so that he could get her head over the sink. It was an odd angle, yet it worked. Running warm water through her hair, he couldn't help but stare into her eyes. Every now and then, she'd turn those stunning eyes onto him. Neither of them made a sound. When her hair was wet, he lathered it up with the shampoo.

She let out a groan as his fingers massaged her scalp.

Rinsing out the soap, he ran his fingers through her hair.

"You're good at this."

"Beginner's luck," he said.

"You've not done this before?"

He shook his head. "No, you're my first." He'd shocked her. Next he lathered the conditioner on her hair, taking his time to work it into her hair. He loved touching her, washing her. Pike didn't want it to stop. There had never been any appeal to washing a woman in the past. He'd fuck them, and fuck them hard, but never actually take the time afterward. He wasn't a cuddling man or much of a talking man.

Mary was changing him. He wanted to be those things for her that he'd failed to be for other women.

"So, partnership huh?"

She smiled, and he hated Mac for being the bastard who'd put it there and not him. There were a hell of a lot of things he was finding that he didn't like lately. He didn't like Mac anywhere near her. It was him, Pike who'd got her that job, not Mac. The fucker hadn't wanted to hire her, but Pike had paid for her.

"What's the matter?" she asked.

"What?"

"You're glaring and looking pretty pissed. There's nothing wrong with my hair, is there?"

"No, baby."

Slowing down washing her hair, he counted to ten inside his head to try to bring himself back into focus. It wasn't Mac's fault that Pike had been an ass and lost an opportunity with her.

Finished with her hair, he unplugged the sink watching the suds disappear. He wrung out her hair, paying careful attention to what he was doing.

With most of the water out of her hair, he grabbed a towel, wrapping it around her head. Pike carried her through to his bedroom, placing her on the bed.

"Can you dry your hair?" he asked.

"Sure. It's my leg that's messed up, not my hands." She leaned forward and started drying her hair. The other towel she wore was still in place. Going to his closet he pulled out a pair of jeans and a shirt. Mary always wore clothes that were a size bigger than she needed. The jeans would fit right around the cast and fall loosely down her other thigh.

Next he grabbed a pair of panties and a bra, matching and sexy. She bound her hair up in the towel as he stood before her.

"I've got more sweatpants."

"Those sweatpants are not helping you get better. They're making you worse. This is who you are, not those sweatpants lying on your ass all day." He tugged the towel from around her chest, using her shock to start working her bra up her arms.

"I can do this."

He ignored her, using the opportunity to caress her breasts. Her nipples budded against his palm. She didn't want him, but her body sure as hell did.

"You're not being fair at all."

"That's okay. Hold my waist."

She held onto his waist as he tugged her up. Locking their fingers together he brought her hand up to his shoulders.

"Hold onto me."

"What are you doing?"

He sank to his knees, and she didn't have a choice but to hold onto him.

"Pike?"

"Lift your leg. You're wearing these sexy red lace panties."

"You're not going to get them up the cast."

"How big do you think this cast is?" he asked.

"It's huge."

"No, it's not." She lifted the foot up, and he hooked the loop over her foot. "Put your foot down and lift the other one." She did as he asked without complaint. He worked the panties up her thighs, over the cast and placed them on her hips. Pike slid his hands over the lace then between her thighs. Standing up, he cupped her pussy, staring into her shocked eyes.

"I made your first time a disappointment and for that I'm sorry."

"Get your hands off me."

"I'm going to have this pussy again." He stroked between the seam of her pussy lips going from her entrance up to her clit, circling her over the fabric.

She didn't push him away, nor did she fight him.

He wondered if she'd even touched herself since he'd been between her thighs.

"You may have my pussy again, Pike, but I can promise you, you won't be the last." She shocked him by gripping the back of his head, tugging on his hair. He stared into her eyes, sliding his fingers past the material of her pussy. She was soaking wet and her clit swollen.

Leaning down, he licked along her lips, groaning when she opened her mouth for him to deepen the kiss. She met him halfway, licking his lips. Moving his fingers down to the entrance of her cunt, he slid a finger deep inside feeling how tight she still was.

"This pussy, this is mine."

"I'm not yours, Pike." She muttered the words against his lips.

"Do you want me to stop?" he asked.

Chapter Five

Did she want him to stop? Mary stared into his eyes as his hand stayed still against her pussy. Two of his fingers were inside her, stretching her with his warmth. Licking her lips, Mary didn't know what to do. She didn't want to be with Mac, but she also didn't want to cave to Pike. She didn't want him to stop either. Her decision was torn between wanting something and not having it.

She craved the need for release, to make her first experience better. At the same time she didn't want Pike to think he had some kind of hold over her.

"I'm not going to fall in love with you."

"I'm not asking you to," he said, gritting his teeth.

"This is not love. I'm not going to fall over myself in love with you. This is sex. Nothing more. You're going to teach me everything you failed on that night."

He arched a brow. "Am I?"

"Yes."

"And why would I do that?"

"Gossip spreads. It wouldn't take long for the brothers of the club to know you can't hack giving a virgin a good time," she said. She could fight fire with fire. Had Pike forgotten where she came from? Where Holly spent Christmases with her parents being loved and cared for by everyone around her, Mary had learned how to disappear. She'd learned how to fight for survival and to take care of herself.

Pike was under some kind of assumption that she was this weak woman who needed him. She didn't need him. What she wanted out of him was sex, that was all. Using him to get what she wanted.

No other man in Vale Valley held her interest. Only Pike.

She could cut her heart out of the equation. He'd broken her heart, torn her life in two. For the last few months she'd not really been living, but she could gain it all back now. This was the new her, the one who'd gladly take his fingers, and relish the orgasm he was going to give her.

"I don't want you to stop."

"You're playing with a master here, Mary. Don't think you won't get burned."

"You fooled me once, Pike. You're not going to fool me again." Reaching down, she touched his cock. He was already aroused, pulsing against her hand with his need. "I know what you want now. I'm not giving you anything else." She rubbed her hand up and down his pants, watching his eyes dilate.

Mary had been a fighter all her life. She knew how to cut people off, shut them out, and deal with life. Pike, he'd gotten through her defenses, torn her apart as he was the only man she'd ever been in love with. No more. She wasn't going to love him anymore. The attraction was there, and she wanted him, her body wanted him. What was wrong with giving in to a little need?

Tugging on his belt, she loosened up his jeans long enough to fit her hand inside. He wasn't wearing any boxers or briefs. Circling her fingers around his cock, she groaned at the way he filled her hand.

"You want me?" she asked, turning the tables on him. She wasn't going to take this lying down. The old her would have been putty in his hand. This time, she wasn't going to be predictable and what she thought he needed.

"What the fuck happened to you?" He held her neck with his thumb playing along her pulse.

"Nothing happened to me, Pike." She shoved his jeans down his thighs until his cock stood out long and proud. Working from the root of his shaft she brought her hand up to the tip to circle his pre-cum.

The panties he'd placed on her were yanked down her thighs. His fingers slid through her wet pussy. When he touched her clit she almost went up in flames.

"Have you had a man since me?" he asked.

Smiling, Mary shook her head. "You don't get to ask that question. I don't want to tell you."

He'd probably fucked hundreds of women since her. She refused to care what he did with his dick. Providing he wasn't infected with some dick rotting disease then she was happy.

"Tell me."

"No." Anything she'd tell her boyfriend or best friend, she wouldn't tell Pike. He was neither. Pike had lost that right months ago when he broke her heart. The best way to heal a broken heart was to get under a new man. She wasn't going to get under a new man but expel the old one from her system. Mary had desired Pike for so long that she wasn't going to pass this opportunity.

"Fine."

He tipped her to the bed, and with her hand wrapped around his cock, Pike didn't have a choice but to join her on the bed. She giggled, noticing how he moved his body away from her leg.

"You want to play?" he asked.

"I thought we were playing." She stroked his cock to emphasize her words.

"Fuck." He growled the word against her neck.

Smiling up at the ceiling, she closed her eyes while touching him. The tip of his cock was soaking wet now from his arousal. With the way he lay on her she couldn't move to touch him.

She tensed up as his fingers skimmed up the inside of her left thigh. His touch was light, teasing.

"You've got to relax, baby." He licked a path from her pulse up to her ear, whispering. "With you tense like this, you can't enjoy what I'm about to do to you."

"What are you about to do to me?" she asked.

One of his hands was tangled in her wet hair, keeping her in place.

"No, you're not in control here, princess. I'm the one in control."

"You like me here, Pike. Your body is betraying you."

"Let's see about yours." His fingers dived into her pussy. She screamed as three fingers stretched her wider than she had been before. "Do you want to be this wet for me, Mary? This pussy, it knows its master."

"You're not my master, Pike, This pussy is going to know a lot of cock after you." She glared up at him, tightening her hold around his cock.

"You're right. It's going to know a lot of my cock."

He stopped all protest from her by kissing her. His tongue slid inside her mouth, reminding her exactly of how long and thick his cock was. He'd be so big and wide.

She was getting wetter by the second imagining him inside her, pounding. Listening to Holly and Duke fuck had messed with her mind.

"I'm going to fuck you every chance I get. Your pussy is going to be so used to my dick you won't be able to think about another man's cock."

She thrust up to meet his fingers, needing him to stop the ache that was building.

Gripping his shoulder, she sank her nails into his flesh at the same time as working his cock. His breath was coming in shallow pants. She loved that he was struggling to stay in control. He was as lost with sexual need as she was.

She gasped when his thumb landed on her clit, moving from side to side. Each touch had her shaking in his arms.

"Soon it will be my cock inside this pussy while you come apart."

Mary didn't let up on her strokes.

"Fuck, baby, I'm so close to losing control."

She stared into his eyes, watching the pleasure cross his face with her touch. Mary didn't look away, staring right back at him as she worked her pussy on his fingers. It had been too damn long since she had an orgasm. She really needed one.

Blast Holly and her sexy life.

If she'd not spent the last week listening to her friend have sex she wouldn't be crazy now.

"Let yourself go, baby. Come for me."

Closing her eyes, she relaxed against his hold, crying out as the edge of bliss that had been teasing her for so long finally came crashing down. She heard Pike growl then felt the splash of his seed on her stomach. Mary didn't stop touching him through her orgasm.

Finally, he held her hand steady. "You've got to stop." He was shaking, and she saw the pain in his eyes.

"Why?"

"I'm a little sensitive. Men get sensitive after an orgasm."

She tilted her head to the side. "It's good to know."

He didn't look away, and Mary kept staring back. No backing down, no letting feelings get involved.

Pike cupped her cheek, but she stopped him by gripping his wrist. "Don't."

"What?" he asked.

"Don't make this about anything more than what it was."

"Mary?"

"No. I made that mistake before." She spoke the words through gritted teeth. "I meant what I said. I'm not falling, and that means no touches like that."

He looked like he wanted to argue. "Fine." He pulled back and looked at her stomach. "I made a mess."

She couldn't move to clean it, as otherwise she'd have been long gone by now.

Pike left her side, grabbing the towel and wiping the white drops of his cum from her stomach. When it was over, he helped her with the panties, jeans, and shirt.

Mary hated him for being right. She finally felt like she was on the road to recovery.

****

Pike was about to brush her hair when banging on his door interrupted them. He didn't like the way things were going. She'd stopped him from cupping her check, and kissing her lips. It was okay. She was hurting from the past, and he could wait. It wouldn't be long until she caved. He knew women and how they ticked. Finding Mary's weak spot would be a walk in the park.

"Are you expecting company?" she asked.

"No."

"Pike, I know you're in there. Mary! Mary!" Holly yelled for her friend.

"I guess we know who's here."

"Help me up," Mary said, holding out her arms for him to take.

This was not how he anticipated this going. He'd expected her to be falling at his feet, wanting what he wanted. Mary, she was different.

Passing her the brush, he'd really wanted to comb her hair. He didn't know why, but seeing her hold the brush knowing he wouldn't get a chance made him angry. Holly had interrupted his moment with Mary.

She took the brush from his hand, and he walked her back to the kitchen. Being in this room would, he hoped, remind her of what he offered her with his home.

"I'll be back with your guardian."

"I wouldn't be mean to Holly. She'd kick your ass," Mary said, smiling at him.

"I'll keep that in mind." Mary was holding back from him. He saw it in her gaze. The way she wasn't open with him, cutting him off from being with her.

Bowing his head at the door, Pike gritted his teeth. He hadn't expected it to be easy, but he'd not expected her to pull away from him. Mary was a loving woman and yet, she wasn't showing him anything. She'd shown him the lust, not the love.

Fuck, love.

No, he didn't love Mary. He cared about her.

"Open up, Pike," Duke said, knocking on the door.

He didn't love Mary, and yet the thought of her finding anyone else to be with left him sick to his stomach. What the hell was that all about?

Lifting his head, he opened the door to find Holly glaring daggers at him.

"Can I help you?" he asked.

"Yeah, you can help me, you shit. Where's Mary? How dare you take her from Mac like that?" She shoved him hard in the chest. Pike didn't move, at which she growled even harder. "Get out of my way!" she demanded when he didn't move an inch.

"Pike, move your ass out of the way before my woman starts stressing." Duke sent out the warning, reminding him of Holly's delicate condition.

"Fine." Pike moved out of the way to watch Holly barrel past him.

"Mary," Holly said, calling her name.

"Well, that didn't go well," Pike said, waiting for Duke to enter.

"I've told her everything is fine. She's worried about Mary being with you." Duke closed the door behind him.

"Is Raoul pissed?"

"Yeah, he's pissed, but the kid made a point."

"Which was?"

"No matter how much I was pissed at him for doing what he did to Holly, he's more than made up for it. I can't vote the kid out."

"I didn't think you were going to."

"I was hoping to. I've been giving him a shit deal. The bastard took everything I dished out without complaint. It was wrong of me. Russ settled the score, and I started it up again. It doesn't make for a good prez. I've let shit go to my head. You all should vote me out."

Pike gripped Duke's shoulder. "It's not going to happen. This is all new for us, and we're all going to get through this. Talk to him. Sit him down and wipe the slate clean. He's not going to go anywhere, and we need him for Diaz and the deals." Pike's only beef with the kid was what he had done to Holly over three years ago on prom night. No man in the Trojans bragged about banging a brother's daughter. Holly had grown up in the club life and deserved something better. Raoul learned from his mistakes, and from what Pike had seen with Mary, he'd kept his hands to himself. Her pussy was still so fucking tight, begging for his cock to slide inside.

"Come on then, tell me about the change of heart with Mary," Duke said.

"Shouldn't we go back to them?" he asked. He couldn't even hear Mary and Holly talking.

"Nah. Leave them to talk it through. Holly needs to know she's okay, and you need to tell me what the fuck is going on."

Moving toward his office, Pike walked toward the window to stare out across the yard. It was overgrowing with weeds. He'd never been a keen gardener. Didn't know shit about plants or where best to put them.

"Well, Pike? What the fuck is going on? One moment you're telling me to butt out of your business with Mary. You don't see her from one week to the next, and then you're here, taking her back to your place."

"I told you the reasons."

"All of those reasons were there before. Why now?" Duke folded his arms over his chest.

"I thought about what you said."

"What about?"

"Finding the right pussy." Pike didn't look away from the garden. He fisted his hands as before him, he saw Mary swollen with a kid, his kid, with another around her feet laughing, perhaps a dog messing around in the background.

"Is Mary the right pussy?" Duke asked.

"I don't know, man. She is, she isn't. I …" He stopped talking to run fingers through his hair. "The only life I've ever understood was this life. We live and die for the club. We breathe the club."

"So."

"People get killed. We lose people that we love."

"I know."

"Mary, she's always been there you know? Like Holly, she's always been in the background, waiting patiently for shit." He pressed his fist to the glass, not breaking it simply resting against the coolness of it. "I fucked her that day when Holly came to you. I walked in, fucked her, and I made it awful." He'd never opened up to anyone. Being in the club, you fought or you died. You didn't let feelings get in the way. The club was at your back for your old lady, but it didn't stop them getting killed. He'd watched Duke take Holly as his old lady for the club to see. No one would let anything happen to Holly. Ever since watching his friend take Holly, he couldn't stop thinking about Mary. She was protected when she had nothing to do with him.

The club, they had enemies, not a lot but some. He didn't want her to ever be at risk of being killed because of him.

"I've been a fucking coward, Duke." He admitted the truth.

"You love her?"

"I don't know. I care about her, but shit. I've not fucked another woman since I've been inside her. I thought I wasn't a one woman man. I fucked it up, and now, I don't know how to reach her."

"Mary's staying with you."

"Yeah, she's here all right, but she's not really here." Pike told him about trying to touch her.

"Damn, you better have washed your fingers before touching me. I don't want another woman's pussy on my hand," Duke said.

"I'm being serious here."

"I can't tell you how to reach Mary. I don't really know her or what she's been through. I will tell you this, if you love her, it's not going to matter how hard you've got to work, you'll work to get her." Duke gripped his shoulder. "I love you like a brother. Holly, she's the world to me. Taking her as my old lady was the best thing I ever did. She's got my kid in her, and I love her. I'm not afraid for the club to know how I feel. It doesn't make you weak to love a woman. What makes you weak is to hide from it like a coward. The man I know as Pike, he wouldn't hide from anything."

Pike hugged his friend, pulling away quickly. Mary, she wasn't going to be easy to bring back to him. She was there and not there, confusing as hell, but it was the only way he could describe it.

"How's Holly? The pregnancy?"

"Everything is fine. I'm following her orders. She doesn't want to tell anyone. To be honest, she's scared. Her mom lost a kid and couldn't have any more. It's made her scared it'll happen to her. I don't know what to do. She's so fucking afraid. Women go through pregnancy all the time with no problems."

"There's nothing you can do." He slapped Duke on the shoulder, offering him support.

"Thanks, man. I needed that."

"No worries. I'm here for you."

Chapter Six

"This place rivals Duke's. Damn, look at this place. Doesn't this remind you of something?" Holly asked, staring around the large room.

Mary chuckled. "This was the design I picked for our own kitchen, remember? I made a whole notebook of everything I wanted and what I wanted to put in it. This is straight out of dreamland for me."

"You don't think Pike found your notebook? This place is fucking freaky."

"Nah, to get my notebooks would have taken effort. Pike's not like that."

"I don't know. I'm starting to get freaky sense on here that Pike's not like you think."

She wasn't going to think much about it. After what just happened in the bedroom, she wasn't entirely sure what to make of him herself.

"What's going on?" Mary asked.

"You're going to ask me that." Holly pulled out a chair, sitting opposite her. "I go home to discover you're not there and Duke's waiting to tell me how Pike took you from Mac."

"Mac gave me partnership at the diner," Mary said, sharing her news with her best friend.

"No way, really?"

"Yes, I'll get to make more decisions and cook a little more."

"Don't give him everything of yourself. Save a bit for us who love you."

Laughing, Mary turned toward the kettle. Holly had put the kettle on the moment she walked into the kitchen.

"Let me make this."

"Have you been to Pike's house before?" Mary asked.

"Never. I've been working all day, and I'm in desperate need of a drink."

"Coffee?"

"No, tea." Holly paused, staring at the cupboard. Mary had noticed that Holly no longer drank coffee even though she was addicted to the stuff.

"When were you going to tell me?" Mary asked.

Holly sighed. "I guess you hate me right now?"

"You must think I'm a lousy friend if you think that was going to make me hate you." Mary rested her chin on her hand.

"I, erm, I wanted to wait just in case."

The tea was placed in front of her. "In case what?"

"In case it didn't work out. I don't want to get my hopes up."

"Well, tell me. I want to hear you say the words to me right now," Mary said.

"I can't, Mary. I wish I could, but I just can't." Tears were glistening in Holly's eyes. Reaching out Mary took her hand.

"You know, Sheila was attacked and that lost her the unborn baby." When Holly made to pull away, Mary wouldn't let her. "You're not going to fall into that same damn trap, I promise you."

"What if it destroys me?"

"Women lose babies all the time, and it's horrible." Tears filled Mary's eyes as she looked at Holly. "But there are a lot of women who have babies. You cannot allow yourself to live like this, Hols. Seriously, you're pregnant. You're pregnant with Duke's baby. You're going to be a mom to a boy or girl." She smiled through her tears. "Stop worrying."

"But what if—"

"If you lose it then it wasn't supposed to be. You and Duke can go ahead practicing for another. Your mom would be so upset right now. You know she would, Hols."

Holly wiped the tears from her face. "Look at you to put it into perspective. I'm supposed to be here offering you support. Not the other way around."

"Yeah, you suck at support. Leave that job to me."

They both laughed.

"Come on, say it, just once."

"I'm pregnant." The words were a whisper. The happiness on Holly's face made it worthwhile.

"See, you've got to stop worrying. You worrying like this could make you lose the baby."

"Shit, Mary."

"Hey, I'm telling you like it is. I love you. You're my sister where it counts. Stop worrying and embrace the fact you're going to have a baby. I'm going to be an aunt."

Holly broke down and started laughing. "You're a nut when you start."

"You love me this way." She pulled Holly in for a hug. "Now, when you're around me I want to hear all of your plans. We've got a nursery to think about, pregnancy exercises to keep you at the top of your game. Will you be finding out if it's a boy or girl?"

"Pike!"

"No, you're not having a Pike."

"Mary, we're not getting past this subject. We're going to talk about Pike and what's going on."

Letting out a sigh, she stared back at her friend. Holly was truly beautiful from the inside out. She had what it took to take on the club to be Duke's old lady. It wasn't easy being an old lady. Mary recalled many nights finding Sheila crying all alone on the couch waiting for Russ to get home. She never told Holly about what she witnessed. What happened between Holly's parents stayed between them.

"Nothing is going on."

"That didn't look like nothing to me. Your cheeks are all flushed, and do you want me to talk to Duke about bringing you back home?"

Mary nibbled on her bottom lip.

"I knew it. Something did happen."

"You're pregnant, and I was going crazy at your place. It's not mine, and Pike had a lot of good arguments for me not being there."

"We had fun."

"We always have fun. I love being around you and Matthew. The sex though, that got old real fast."

"Sex?" Holly asked, going a nice shade of crimson.

"Yeah, all night long. I mean seriously, what did you expect me to do? You were fucking all the time. It was hard for a girl to get some sleep. I couldn't do anything without hearing you moan Duke's name."

"God, I'm so sorry."

"I've heard how you sound when you orgasm, Holly. It's one time too bloody many. I've heard you come more times than I have." Mary pressed a hand to her chest.

"Crap, Matthew."

"That kid is a genius. He gave me a music player to drown you out."

"I can't face him again." Holly put her hands on her cheeks looking mortified.

"You don't have to worry. Matthew's not going to make you embarrassed. Just don't bring it up."

"We're getting way off subject here. What about you and Pike?"

Thinking about the way he touched her brought heat to her cheeks at the memory.

"I'm going to stay here a while."

"What's going on?" Holly asked.

"Nothing is actually going on, but you could say I'm exploring something with him."

Holly tilted her head to the side. "You do remember he broke your heart?"

"Yes, I remember. I was there. He's not going to get the chance to break it this time." Mary nibbled her lip. "I'm not going to be blinded by feelings or what I think I can have with him. I know what he's offering. I'm not expecting anything more from him."

Holly smiled at her friend. "I want to be here. I want to know what it's all about."

"What, what is all about?"

Licking her lips, Mary took her friend's hands. "That night you called him, we had sex, okay? You know we had sex. It was awful, and he said some things that broke my heart. Listening to you and Duke, I want to know what that is like. To be with someone who makes me scream no matter where I am."

"What about Mac? He's safe."

"I'm safe with Pike. I don't know. He's not going to hurt me, and I'm not going to let him hurt me."

"You've been in love with Pike."

"He was a crush. I know the difference."

Holly looked at her doubtfully. "I don't think it's just a crush."

"Trust me. If it all goes wrong, you'll be the first person I go to for a shoulder to cry on."

"I love you, Mary. I'll kick his ass if he hurts my girl."

She hugged Holly. "I'm not going to get hurt. You need to start thinking happy thoughts about being pregnant. I want to see you happy, not sad."

"Is it okay to come in now?" Pike asked, calling through to the kitchen.

"I don't know," Mary said, smiling at Holly. "Is it?"

"He can come in."

Turning in her seat she watched Duke follow in behind Pike.

"I'm pregnant," Holly said, obviously stunning both men. "You're right, it's good to finally say it."

Duke moved to Holly's side. Mary couldn't look away as he cupped her cheek, tilted her head back, and claimed her lips. "I love you, baby."

"We've got company."

"I don't care." Duke proceeded to kiss her, or a better way to describe it was devour Holly's mouth.

"Okay, this is not something I need to see. I've just gotten away from the sound of you two screwing. Please, give me a break." Mary slapped a hand over her mouth. All three turned toward her. "Sorry, I don't know where that came from."

"I always knew you had a mouth on you," Pike said.

Mary chuckled, happy for her friend.

****

"I'm not sleeping with you. You can forget it," Mary said, glaring at Pike.

Standing in his bedroom, he stared at Mary in the silk negligee he'd picked out. She clearly didn't know the lace showed off her beautiful tits to perfection. He'd have to invest in more negligees even though he preferred her to be naked.

"You're sleeping in that bed beside me. No arguments."

"You're completely insane. Did you just wake up and decide it was time to torture me?" she asked.

"Nope. You need to be cared for. I don't trust you not to get up off your feet and start moving around."

"You idiot. You took my crutches. I'm not looking to be stuck here any longer than I have to be."

He had another plan for her staying. Mary wasn't getting away, and he was going to fight her every step of the way.

"My leg is in a cast. You bang it up with your body, it's going to hurt."

"I'm not going to bang it up."

She grabbed a pillow and threw it at him. "Stop being so argumentative. Why can't I have my own room?"

"Because I want you in this one."

"Do you always get what you want?" She folded her arms underneath her breasts.

"Let's see. I wanted to take care of you at my place, check, you're here. I wanted to wash you and clean you so you didn't stink." She growled at him, reaching for another pillow, which he dodged. "Check, you no longer stink. I got you in clothes that were right for you, even if they're a size too big. You're not a size twenty, Mary. Stop dressing like it."

"You're evil. How dare you?"

She scrambled for another pillow. With her distracted, he tackled her to the bed, paying careful attention not to bump her leg. He didn't want to hurt her. Grabbing her hands, he pressed them beside her head to stop her from clawing his eyes out.

"Yes, I get what I want. You're going to sleep because I like taking care of you." Placing both of her hands above her head, he slid his hand down her body. "I can make you feel good, Mary."

He slid his hand down to her breast, pushing the lace of the negligee aside to stroke her nipple. She groaned, but Pike knew he hadn't won, not by a long shot. Mary wanted nothing to do with him other than sex. He couldn't change her mind instantly, but over time, he was going to. She was his woman. Talking to Duke had made it all clear in his mind.

For a short time he'd be happy to be used by her, but he wasn't going to let her go even when her leg was better.

"If you don't want me to touch you I'll go to a different bed." He brought his fingers up the inside of her thigh, touching over her pussy. Pike was starting to wonder why he even bothered trying to put panties on her. Every time he got her in panties all he wanted to do was tear them off her body. "Should I go or should I stay?"

"Don't you dare leave!" She touched his hand over her mound, keeping him in place.

"Do you want me to touch you?" he asked.

"No. I want you to fuck me. I want you to make this time more memorable than ever before. I don't want you to stop."

He stared into her eyes.

"This isn't love. I want what Holly has when she fucks Duke."

"I've never fucked Duke."

She hit his arm.

He placed his hand on the cast, running the tips of his fingers up and down her thigh. She'd been hurt trying to protect Holly. The only pleasure he got was from knowing that the men who'd hurt her were dead. They were all dead.

"I don't like you being hurt."

"If I wasn't hurt then I wouldn't be here."

He smiled. "I'm not going to complain about you being here. I've got to be careful about your leg."

"You need to use a condom."

"I didn't last time."

"We got lucky."

"What?"

"I wasn't pregnant. I didn't think about it until afterward."

Pike hadn't even given a thought about pregnancy. "Did you take anything to stop it?"

"No, I'm not taking anything now. You've got to wear a condom. I don't want to get pregnant with your kid."

Her comment was a punch to the gut. There was a time when Mary would have wanted anything he'd give. After seeing an image of her pregnant in the garden, he'd not been able to get it out of his mind. She'd look so damn beautiful, perfect.

"I'll wear a condom." He couldn't push her now. Mary was still struggling with what he did to her.

"Do you have one?" she asked.

"Yes."

He reached toward the bed, grabbing out a pack of condoms.

"Do you bring women here often?"

"Never. I always keep a supply. I'd rather be safe." He pulled out two condoms, tearing the foil wrapping on one, and sliding it over his dick. "I'm nothing if not prepared."

She chuckled.

The noise turned into a moan as he tugged her panties down her thighs with his teeth. When the edge of the panties got to her cast he changed to his hands, removing them completely off.

"I'm going to be careful with your leg. The moment the cast comes off, we can have a lot of fun."

"What makes you think I'm going to want you when the cast comes off?"

"Baby, I've not even started. You're going to be screaming and begging for me." He pushed the edge of the negligee up her thighs, exposing her pussy to his gaze. "Now that's what I call beautiful."

She had a light dusting of hair. He'd never been into women who completely shaved it off.

"Do you think I should shave it off?" she asked. "I tried it once. Hurt like hell afterwards."

Skimming his fingers through her curls, he smiled. "Darling, I can promise you, I don't have any problem with you like this. I like my woman to look exactly like that, a woman." He gripped some of the hair on her mound. "This is what I like."

She gasped as he tugged on the fine hairs.

Pike slipped his fingers through her slit. She was soaking wet, and he teased her swollen clit, caressing over the nub.

Mary arched up against him.

Pressing a kiss to her stomach, he inhaled her musky scent.

"What are you doing?"

"I'm going to eat this pussy. It has been too damn long since I've had my lips on you."

The light cast from the lamp put her in perfect view.

"Now, look at this sweet little pussy." He opened her lips and stared at her wet cunt. His mouth watered, and he couldn't resist swiping his tongue from her entrance up to her clit. Circling the bud, he moved down to plunge inside her.

"So fucking tasty," he said, muttering the words against her clit.

"Pike!" She screamed his name as he sucked her clit into his mouth.

Mary reared up on the bed. Her fingers sank into his hair, and she rubbed herself over his face.

"Yeah, that's it, baby, get off on me."

"Shut up," she said.

Untangling her hands from his hair, Pike pressed her to the bed. He was hard as fucking rock.

"You're not going to get me to shut up now, darling. I'm going to talk and tell you exactly what I'm doing to you."

Locking her hands above her head within one of his, he gripped his length with the other, finding her center. Staring into her brown eyes, Pike slammed to the hilt, not taking his time, and giving her every inch of his cock.

"Fuck, you're so tight. This is what I've been dreaming about since the first time."

She cried out but couldn't touch him as he kept her in place.

"I can feel every little pulse of your cunt, baby. Your body betrays your need for me. You may not love me or even like me, yet your body, she likes me. I like your body."

With his hands on hers, it held him off her body. He stroked her tits, pinching her nipples. The touch had her tightening around his cock, and he groaned.

"This body is perfect for me."

"It's not yours."

He pulled out of her only to pound back inside, roughly. She cried out at the invasion.

"Your body has a different idea." Pike watched her come apart, loving every emotion that crossed her face. She looked so beautiful in the way she gave herself to him. "I'm going to fuck you, Mary. This pussy, it's not going to want any other cock. You're going to be screaming out for me."

Pike pulled out and slammed back inside, over and over again. He took her to the edge of bliss yet kept her there, refusing to give her any more. Reaching between them, he touched her clit, stroking her as he slid inside her.

"You're so damn wet for me. When this cast comes off, I'm going to show you a whole new side to what you'll love." He was going to show her shit that she didn't even think she wanted. "Come for me, Mary. Come all over my cock."

She cried out, shaking as her cum washed over his cock. The condom stopped him from feeling it, but the tightening of her pussy was sheer heaven. Gritting his teeth, he held back his own orgasm to enjoy hers. The sweet sounds coming from her mouth were beautiful to hear.

"Now, it's my turn."

He fucked her hard, making her take every single inch of his length. Pounding inside her, Pike found his own release. Wrapping his arms around her, Pike groaned out, loving the feel of her. This is what it meant to own a pussy. No other man had been here before, only him.

He was going to keep her that way.

****

"Fuck, man, this party is wild," Daisy said.

Raoul couldn't agree more, gripping the waist of the woman riding his cock on the dance-floor. He was fully clothed, yet this woman was seriously dry humping him.

Daisy had two women surrounding him, touching him. The club was thriving with sexual activity, every man and woman begging for sex.

"Do you want to get out of here?" the blonde asked, licking his earlobe.

"Sure thing, babe." Raoul gave Daisy the nod that he was taking the woman out back to fuck.

"Wet that dick, man."

Chuckling, he took the lead, driving out of the back of the club. They entered a darkened alleyway. Pushing the woman up against the wall, Raoul sucked on her neck. He didn't kiss any of the bitches that were just plain old fucks.

"Don't you want to know my name?" she asked.

"I don't need to."

He grabbed a condom out of his pocket, opening his jeans, Raoul was about to take his cock out when a feminine cry filled the air.

"Please, let me go. I don't want this. Ouch, leave me alone."

Raoul frowned. That was not the sound of a woman wanting any fun.

"Baby, what's the matter?" the blonde asked.

"Get back inside."

"I want you to fuck me. How can you fuck me if I'm inside?"

Pocketing the condom, he glared at the blonde. "Get the fuck back inside. I'll deal with you in a minute. Tell Daisy I need his ass outside." Zipping up his jeans, he shoved her back through the door, and he took a step toward the scuffling.

"You just shut your fucking mouth, slut. You want cock. I'll give you cock."

He hated men who didn't take no for an answer. Rounding the corner there was enough light from the street light on the other side of the wall for him to see what was going on. There was a young woman, not even twenty, held trapped against the wall. Tears were streaming down her face. There was not a smidge of makeup on her. She was beautiful. Raoul saw it instantly even with the fear in her eyes. Her beauty was refreshing, natural. She had long glossy red hair, startling green eyes, and a figure fit for a fifties actress when fuller was better.

Any sign of arousal he felt was diminished as he spotted not one but four men holding her against her will.

"Let me go," she said.

"No. I'm going to fuck this nice tight pussy and then my friend here is going to. By the time we're done, you're going to love fucking many men."

She struggled against their hold. She whimpered, crying out as they touched her.

"You know, I hate men who can't take no for an answer," Raoul said. He didn't need to see any more to know he was interrupting a rape.

The four men turned to him.

"Please, help me."

When the four men saw it was just him they got cocky. He was in the dark so they didn't see the leather cut he wore.

"Find your own slut to fuck. This one's ours."

"No, she's not. She doesn't want you, and you're going to step the fuck away from her now."

"Or what?" The one who'd touched her sex stepped forward. "What are you going to do? There's one of you and four of us."

Raoul smirked, stepping into the light. Their gazes moved to his jacket taking in the sight of his patch.

That's right, fuckers. You're about to enter hell.

"Please, I don't want this. I never wanted this," the woman said.

"Shut it." The man holding her arm slapped her around the face.

"Look, man, we don't want any trouble—"

"You're going to get trouble. A shitload of trouble." He brought his fists up, smiling at them. "The only question now? Which one is going to come for an ass whooping first?"

"I'll deal with this loser," the blond said, charging toward him.

Slamming his fist into the man's face, Raoul knocked him on his ass, and the fight was on. The three other men charged at him at once. At the same time, Daisy fell out of the door.

"Fuck, the real party started without me."

One by one they charged at the men, taking two on each. Out of the corner of his eye, Raoul saw the woman cower on the ground. Slamming his fist into faces and stomach, he took them down, hating the fear the bastards created. Within minutes all four men were knocked out on the floor.

"Fuck, man, you're awesome. I'm so telling the guys you know how to party."

Raoul walked toward the woman. She looked up at him, terrified.

"They told me my friend was waiting out here," she said. Her lip was wobbling. "I don't drink. I don't do anything wrong."

"They're assholes. They're not going to hurt you."

He touched her shoulder, and she whimpered. Pulling her into his body, Raoul inhaled her vanilla scent, shocked by how much he liked the smell clinging to her skin. "I'm not going to hurt you. I promise. I'm not like them."

"Okay."

"I'm Raoul, and that big lug is Daisy." He pointed behind him. Her gaze went behind him to land on Daisy.

"Hello."

"What's your name, honey?" Daisy asked.

"It's Zoe." She looked between the men.

"You're safe. Neither of us is into force."

"No, damn, I like my pussy willing," Daisy said.

"How old are you?" Raoul asked.

"I'm twenty. I was supposed to be picking up my friend from this bar. She promised she'd be waiting." Zoe sniffled. "I'm sorry."

"I'm going to take you home."

"Okay," Zoe said, gripping his hand.

He really didn't like how much she held onto him or how much his body liked her. Zoe had brought a reaction from him that no woman ever had before.

Chapter Seven

Three weeks later

"How are you holding up?" Holly asked, taking a seat at Pike's table.

Mary smiled, thinking about the last three weeks of living with Pike. She'd not seen anyone besides Holly or Duke. Pike wouldn't allow Mac or anyone else to enter his home. She didn't mind and loved the protective way he was being. At the same time, she didn't allow him to get too close. When she woke up to find him holding her, she'd move away.

"From that smile I say everything is going well?"

Holly rested her chin on her hands, raising a brow.

"We're having sex. We're having a lot of sex," Mary said. Her cheeks were heating under Holly's watchful gaze.

"But?"

"I won't let it go any further." Mary looked down at her cast. They were restricted to what they could do sexually, but Pike had a big imagination.

"How can it not be going any further? You've had sex, right? That's as far as it can go."

Mary bit her lip. "It's not just about the sex. I, erm, I won't let him cuddle me or kiss me unless we're having sex. There have been times I'm standing around the kitchen because the doctor said I could, and he'll come up behind me, wrapping his arms around me. I tell him not to. I can't do it, Hols. I can't let him have that part of me."

"You're having sex without the commitment?"

"What do you think I should do?" Mary stared at her friend hoping she'd have some insight. "I mean, he's being really sweet." She pointed across the kitchen to the book stand he'd built for her. "He did all of that for me. Have a look around. He's packed the kitchen with my own stuff."

"I think he's trying to tell you something," Holly said, turning back to face her.

"My cast is coming off in a couple of days. The doctor told me the rest was just a precaution, but everything is looking good. I went to the hospital the other day."

"I know. I've been waiting to find out what went on at your appointment. Pike's pretty protective of you." Holly took a sip of her coffee. Getting to her feet, Mary walked toward the drawer where she'd stored the notebook she found. "Should you be walking around?"

"I've got some mobility. Honestly, it doesn't even hurt to move anymore." She handed the book to Holly.

"What's this?"

"Have a look." She'd found the notebook the other day. It was full of notes on everything she'd made a note of herself.

"I don't understand. This is your giant wish list. I remember you writing this."

"I know. I remember, and you remember. It was in Pike's office drawer."

"What were you doing going through his office drawer?" Holly asked. "You know they don't like you snooping."

"I'm not a fucking rat or a snitch, Hols. I was looking for a pen. I couldn't find a working one, and he wasn't around. I found this, and I couldn't help but look."

"What do you think it is?"

"I think he somehow got into our apartment and found my wish list."

"This is a good thing, Mary."

"How? He can break into our apartment, our private space, but he can't give me two minutes of niceness after he took my fucking virginity." She dropped down into her chair. "Do you even think I'd be here if not for this stupid leg? I'd not even seen him for weeks."

"You danced with him at my wedding."

"I didn't have a choice. I wasn't going to hurt you because I didn't like him." Mary tucked some hair behind her ear. Pike spent a great deal of time washing and brushing her hair. The moments where he took care of her were the ones she cared for most, and yet, they were the ones she hated.

"You're going to fight him every step of the way?"

Tears filled her eyes, and she growled out her frustration. "Crap, I refuse to cry over that man."

"You've been in love with him all of your life, Mary. I don't think that's just going to stop because you demand it."

"I do demand it. I don't want to be having these feelings for anyone, least of all Pike. He broke my heart, and I'm not going to let him stamp all over me again."

Holly reached out to take her hand. "You've got to do what makes you happy. I love you, you're my best friend, and you're so going to be the godmother to my child so that I can spend quality time with my man."

"Really?"

"Yeah. Duke and I have already talked about it. We think you and Pike would be awesome together."

"Ugh, there's no getting away from him."

Holly chuckled. "That usually happens when you're determined *not* to love someone. I was talking to Duke, and he told me Pike hasn't been around the club much. He goes to the meets, does what he's ordered, and leaves."

Mary *had* noticed he was home a lot more. When she and Holly shared an apartment, they could go a couple of days before they saw each other if their lives got busy. Now, she saw Pike every single day. She saw him when she woke up in the morning, at breakfast, sometimes at lunch, and he was always home for dinner, then at night. Nights were her favorite, yet they were the moments she hated as well. Every time he touched her, she wanted to give in and submit more than her body to Pike. He showed her each time everything he'd failed to give her that night all those weeks ago. She'd come more under his hands than any other time.

"Shoot, I better go. I love you, Mary." Holly got to her feet.

Following her friend toward the front door, Mary saw her out, and she was alone in the large house. Hobbling to the kitchen, she was washing up the cups when the door went again. Pike let himself in so it couldn't be him.

Walking to the door, Mary smiled. Mac stood on the other side.

"Hey," she said. It had been three weeks since she'd last seen him. "You've not come to tell me my job is going, are you?"

"No. You're my partner." He pulled something from behind his back. "I came to see how my best girl was doing." He held a large bouquet of roses. The blooms were a deep red.

"They're beautiful."

"Oh, they're not for you. I just used them as bribery to get past the door," he said.

She chuckled, taking the flowers from him. "Do you want to come in?" Mac really was a good friend.

"Is Pike in? He'll kick my ass."

"No. He's out at the moment. Come on." She opened the door for him.

"You're on your foot."

"Yeah, I'm going to the doctor in a couple of days. He believes everything is fine for me to now have the cast completely removed." She didn't doubt that was up to Pike. The first few weeks at his place and he'd bossed her around, not letting her do anything but rest.

"Who would have thought Pike had it in him to take care of you?"

"I sure didn't. I still can't believe he likes me."

Mac stood in the kitchen as she filled the kettle. "Here, let me get that." He took the kettle from her, placing a hand on her waist.

Mary tensed up. She'd never gotten close to Mac. He'd offered her dates, which she'd declined at first. After Pike screwed her in more ways than one, she had gone on a couple of dates with Mac, but she'd never done anything keeping her own space. They were friends, and it wasn't ever going to be anything more.

"I've missed you, Mary."

"What are you doing?" she asked.

He placed the kettle behind her. The moment his hand was free, he cupped her cheek.

"You're a brilliant cook, and you know how to make a business work."

"I said I'd be your partner." She placed her hands on his chest, wanting to push him off.

"And I look forward to us working together."

The sound of a gun cocking had her turning toward the sound. Pike stood with his gun pointed at Mac.

"I suggest you get your fucking hands off her."

"Pike?" Mary asked, shocked by the anger on his face.

"I told you to stay the fuck away, Mac."

Mac let her go, and Mary used the counter to hold herself up. "And I didn't exactly listen to instructions."

"You're going to leave and forget about this partnership crap. Mary's not doing it."

"That's not your call to make," Mary said, angry that he was taking over her life.

"You can't stop the partnership."

Neither of the men was watching her.

"I can't? Why don't you tell her who's been paying for her job, huh? Why don't you tell Mary who persuaded you to give her a job?"

"What?" Mary asked, looking from one man to the other.

"Why don't you tell her who it was that told you to try one of her pies?"

Looking from Mac to Pike, Mary saw the truth on Mac's face. "You weren't going to employ me?"

"The diner wasn't doing so well. I couldn't just fucking give you a job."

"Who paid for my job? The club?" Mary asked, looking toward Pike.

"No, I paid for your job. I gave Mac your salary along with a little extra."

"I stopped doing it."

"You've denied two payments, asshole. That doesn't mean you stopped it."

Mary rubbed at her temples, unable to comprehend what the hell was going on.

"Pike paid for your job, and yes, he wanted me to keep an eye on you, but everything changed. I do like you, Mary, as a friend."

She looked at Pike, shaking her head.

"I've been taking care of you for a long time," Pike said.

"No, you better shut the fuck up." Mary slashed her hand across the air in front of her. "You're both liars. How dare you? Was the partnership a payoff?"

"No, I was offering you that. I want us to be a team. The diner is thriving. We're going strong. I want to share it all with you. We're good together, and I care about you, but I'm not going to pretend that there's something there between us. We're friends. The partnership was my idea. You've got all the ideas, Mary, and I respect them where I once did not."

"You're a liar, Mac," she said, tears falling down her cheeks. She noticed he said care, not love. They were friends, or at least she thought they were. "You didn't want me to work for you as a waitress?"

"In the beginning no, but ..."

"But what?"

"Pike asked me to take care of you."

She didn't know what to do or say.

"Get out now before I fucking shoot you," Pike said.

Looking at Pike, she waited for Mac to leave. He didn't put up a fight, and she didn't expect him to. She and Mac were never going to be anything more than friends and business partners, if she could deal with this latest revelation.

The sound of the door closing made her flinch.

"I don't get what you're doing," she said. "You hated me."

"I never hated you."

"You've been paying for me to work?"

"Yes."

His jaw clenched in anger.

"I can't believe you've done this, you've been doing this." Running fingers through her hair, she stared around the kitchen. "Since the moment I left high school you've been there."

"Yes."

"And you treated me like shit all these years."

"Yes."

She shook her head as the tears started to fall. "I can't do this now."

"You're not going back to your apartment," he said.

Mary turned back to look at him. "What?"

"I've been emptying out your apartment. There's nothing left of it. You're staying here, and Mac stays away."

"There's nothing there. We're friends because of you, asshole. Not me. You pushed us together. Mac only cares about me. It's not love. We're friends."

She slammed her hand against the wall. Her anger built to a fever pitch. "You're not coming near me. I mean it." She walked away, going straight to the spare bedroom.

What the hell was she to do with this information?

****

One week later Pike stormed around his home getting angrier than ever. Mary had left his home without him. The cast on her leg was gone, and she was already out with her independence.

Pulling out his cell phone he dialed Holly's number. The last week since he'd caught Mac in his home had been a fucking nightmare. Mary wouldn't let him near her. The day she was due to get her cast off, she'd called Russ to take her to the hospital. Pike had been pushed aside. She didn't talk to him, look at him, or even answer him. Mary had cut him off completely, and he hated it. All of his hard work had gone to shit because of that fucker Mac.

"Hello," Holly said, giggling. "Stop it, Duke."

"Come here, beautiful. I want that pussy one more time."

"Stop it."

"Where's Mary?" Pike asked, growling the words.

"Pike?"

"No, it's fucking Santa Claus."

"Very funny. Mary, she's back at the diner working. She told me yesterday she was taking the breakfast shift that needed for her to be in the diner at six."

"Fucking piece of shit," Pike said, hanging up.

She'd kept him out of her business, and now he was pissed. Mac hadn't even been in touch. Slamming out of his house, he made his way toward his bike. Putting on his jacket, he straddled his bike, turning it over. The vibration of the machine did little to calm his anger. He wanted to hurt someone, fuck them over, and have the satisfaction of breaking bones. Revving his engine, he rode toward the diner in time. With every mile he rode, the angrier he got.

The last few weeks had been perfect. She wouldn't let him close, but she allowed him into her body. Mary cut him off every chance he tried to get closer to her.

What did you expect? You hurt her, and she's not the kind of woman to take that shit.

Riding up to the diner, he got off his bike. The diner was full with the breakfast customers. He didn't give a shit.

Storming into the back of the diner he found Mac flipping bacon while Mary stood beside him, helping. She didn't have her cast on. Her pale thighs peeked out of her waitressing uniform. The uniform was a horrible pastel blue dress that hugged under her breasts. It didn't complement Mary's figure at all. What also didn't help was the fact she made sure to wear it a size bigger. Everything she owned was a size bigger than she needed.

Without waiting for them to notice him, he walked up to Mary, grabbing her arm and leading her to the office.

"Pike, this is my diner," Mac said.

"This is my fucking woman. Don't get involved or I'll put a bullet in your head." He entered the office, slamming the door behind, and locking it.

"What the hell do you think you're doing?" Mary tugged her arm out of his hold, glaring at him. He dropped the blinds so they were in privacy. "I can't believe you're doing this."

"I wake up this morning to discover you're gone."

"So."

"You've not long had the cast removed from your leg and you're already working."

"The doctor said I could go straight back to work. I don't need to rest. I've been on rest for so long. I'm fine."

Pike shook his head. "You should have told me."

"No, I shouldn't. We're not a couple."

"You're living in my house—"

She stepped closer to him, shoving him hard. He didn't move.

"I didn't have a choice. I've talked to the landlord of my apartment. You canceled everything. I've got nowhere else to live right now. I'd be elsewhere if I could."

"You're mine, Mary."

"No, I'm not. Stop with all your possessive male shit."

"My dick's been inside you. You're mine."

Mary slapped him around the face. "Don't you dare say that shit to me. I would have been yours, but you lost that right. You lost that chance."

He cupped her cheek, wrapping his other hand around her waist to pull her close. "That's where you're wrong." Pike slammed his lips down on hers to silence any protest. "I hurt you, and I know that. I can't change what happened, but I'm going to make it better for you. I promise." Stroking a thumb across her cheek, Pike plundered his tongue into her mouth, silencing her. He pushed her back toward the desk. The nice neat desk that she'd cleaned. Lifting her up onto the desk, her hands gripped onto his shoulders as he pushed up her dress.

One week he'd been without her, and he couldn't last another second without her warm heat surrounding his shaft.

"Your pussy is mine. No one is going to know how warm and tight you are." He tore the panties she wore, pocketing them. Unzipping his jeans, he pulled out his cock, putting a condom on quickly.

"Please, Pike, please," she said.

He tugged her to the edge of the desk, running the tip of his cock through her wet heat before slamming it all the way inside her.

Growling, he held onto her waist tightly as her warmth surrounded him. One day he'd be inside her without the condom. He couldn't wait for that moment. Until then, he'd have to use a condom.

He had to gain her trust that he lost.

"Move, Pike, I need to … to…"

"Tell me what you need, Mary. Tell me what you want." Claiming her lips, he stopped her from telling him what she wanted. Slowly he withdrew from her pussy and glanced down to see his latex covered cock. The condom was slick with her cream, and he didn't stop, pushing back inside her.

"I need you to fuck me and to do it hard."

"Your wish is my command." Pulling out of her, he yanked her off the desk, turning her over so that her beautiful ass was in the air.

"What are you doing?"

He stroked his hand over the delicate globes. "We couldn't do this with your cast. I didn't want to do anything that would hurt you." Opening her legs slightly, he ran his cock through her pussy lips, coating the shaft with more of her cream. When he was at the entrance, he glided his hand up her back to grip her neck. "Now I can." He rammed inside her growling as she screamed. Mac and Ron would hear what he was doing to her. "You can be mad at me. Hate me, scream at me all you want, Mary, but I can give you this." He swiveled his hips, going deeper inside her. Slipping his free hand between her thighs, he stroked over her clit, using everything to his advantage. "I can show the entire fucking world and have you screaming out in orgasm every night."

"What … what do you want?" she asked, breathlessly.

"I'll take your attitude and I'll take your hate, but every night you're in my bed, fucking my cock."

"You're not getting anything else. I don't forgive you for taking over my life, and I don't forgive you for hurting me." She cut off as he pinched her clit.

"Do we have a deal?" He'd work on getting her to fall back in love with him. It wouldn't be easy, but then nothing in life was ever easy. Fighting for love was damned hard, and in the end, it would all be worth it. She would be his woman.

"Deal."

"Then Mac is nothing to you other than a business partner."

"Yes."

Bringing her to orgasm, Pike slammed inside her finding his own release within seconds.

Collapsing over her, he kissed the back of her neck.

"Get out of me," she said, tensing underneath him.

"What?"

"You've had your fun. Get out."

Pike gritted his teeth. This he hated more than anything. She wouldn't allow him the chance to get close to her. He could fuck her, but nothing else.

"Mary?"

"I've got work to do. I'll be home at some point tonight."

"What the fuck do you mean some point tonight?" he asked, angrier. He withdrew from her body. Removing the condom, he watched her smooth down her uniform then bind her hair back into place.

"I've got stuff to do. You're not going to own me."

"I've owned you a long time."

She smiled. "And you lost that right. I've got to work."

"You're still working here?"

"Yes. I know you don't like it, but I do like working here. There's nothing you can do to stop me."

Throwing the used condom into the trash, he zipped up his jeans. "Fine." Opening the office door he walked over toward Mac. Slamming his fist into the guy's face, he slammed him up against the wall.

"Whoa, fuck," Ron said in the background.

"You touch her, you die. You do anything to hurt her, you die. She's mine."

"Are you claiming her?"

"She's mine. That's all your ass needs to know. You're not a Trojan. I am. Mary, she's mine." He was saying a lot of that lately.

"I haven't touched her, Pike," Mac said.

"Leave him alone," Mary said, coming to the door.

Pike wrapped his fingers around Mac's neck. Nothing would give him greater pleasure than seeing him dead.

Mary placed her hand on his arm. "You've not got a right to want him dead. You made him important."

This was all his fault. Releasing his hold, he grabbed Mary, slamming his lips down on hers. He made sure he did it in complete view of the customers in the diner. "I'll see you tonight."

Putting his sunglasses on, he left the diner, angry as shit. He rode his bike to the clubhouse, parking up, and slamming through the doors.

"What the fuck is your problem?" Duke asked, looking up from the papers in his hands. One of the mechanics, Billy, stood beside him. Billy was eighteen, young, temperamental, and begging to be part of the club.

"Do I need a fucking reason?" He stormed over to the bar taking a seat. Daisy was sitting at the bar with Raoul. The clubhouse went silent as Pike vibrated with anger. He wanted to hurt someone or something.

"So, rumor mill has it you've got the sexy little Mary staying with you," Daisy said.

It was the wrong thing to say or do. Pouncing on Daisy, Pike started ramming his fists into any available flesh.

Daisy wasn't a kind man. Within seconds they were fighting around the clubhouse. Several of the whores, including Baby, were jumping out of the way.

Pushing Daisy against a table, Pike gripped the man's jacket to throw him against something else. Daisy stalled him, slamming him into the wall.

"When I say stop, I fucking mean stop." Duke pushed in between them, holding both men apart. There was no use fighting Duke. The moment they did, he'd put them down. Duke didn't earn his right to be president by being a pussy. During his anger and lashing out at Daisy, Duke had ordered them to stop. "What the fuck?"

"Ask him," Daisy said. "He's gone off the fucking deep end. Last I checked Mary was free fucking pussy. No one had claimed that shit."

Pike lunged. Duke kept him still.

"You stay still. You don't get to fucking move right now, Pike." Duke stared at each of them. "I'm going to lower my hands. If one of you even fucking blinks you'll be doing toilet duty for the next month. Neither of you will get near pussy."

Slowly, Duke lowered his hands. Standing tall, Pike forced himself to stay still. He wouldn't back down or go anywhere else to ruin his chance of being with Mary. No pussy meant sticking to the club, and he wouldn't do that. His relationship with Mary was hanging on by a thread.

"I heard what Daisy said. Mary—are you claiming her?" Duke asked.

"I can't, not yet," Pike said. He'd claim her in a heartbeat.

"What?" Daisy asked.

Within seconds the brothers took notice. It wasn't unheard of for the brothers to bring in new whores to share. Claiming a woman, it was rare, especially for an old lady. Holly was the first woman to be claimed in over five years.

"You're making Mary your old lady?" Raoul asked, stepping closer.

"Yes." He spoke the words through gritted teeth.

"I take it she doesn't know that," Holly said. All the brothers turned to look at the woman who'd entered the clubhouse. "You told me to meet you here, Duke."

"It's okay. What's said in the club stays in the club. You'll not repeat any of this shit to Mary."

"I won't even though she's my best friend." Holly glared at him, and Pike stared right back. "You better make sure she knows your intentions."

"I will."

"You've got a battle on your hands. Mary refuses to let you close. I'll be in your office." She touched Duke's shoulder on the way past.

"You better know what you're doing," Duke said. "No more fights in my club."

When Holly came, Duke went to play.

Within minutes Pike was calm, his aggression finally gone from attacking Daisy.

"I'm sorry, man," Pike said.

"No, I didn't know you were going to claim her. Next time keep us informed of what you're doing with your woman. You've been determined not to for so long," Daisy said. Pike shook Daisy's hands. "Holly's right, though. You've got a battle on your hands."

"It's a battle I'm going to win."

Chapter Eight

Mary was tired. She was attending the gym in the city, and it was the first time since her leg being broken that she'd been able to do anything. Turning over a new leaf was damned hard to do. She hated looking at all the skinny women who were talking about all the weight they were going to lose. None of them needed to lose weight. They were skin and bones. What she hated more was the way they talked about how much they weighed. She'd done everything in her power to ignore them. It was hard to do.

Were they the kind of women Pike preferred?

Comparing herself to those women, Mary couldn't help but to come up short. All of her life she'd been bigger. It was a miracle that she'd become friends with Holly as Mary was a little bigger even than Holly. She was sticking to her healthy eating and her lifestyle choice. However, she was starting to doubt the gym.

Pushing those thoughts away, she entered Pike's house, crying out as she was shoved against the wall.

"Where have you been?" He held onto her neck. She'd dropped the keys onto the floor and gasped out.

"What the hell?"

"Where have you been?"

He wasn't hurting her. His breath fanned across her face. She closed her eyes, trying to stop the flood of arousal working its way around her body. In her mind she envisioned the women at the gym. Their tanned firm flesh without an ounce of fat on them.

"I was out."

"Were you with another man?"

"What? No."

"Tell me."

"I just did!" She yelled out the answer. He quickly turned her, lifting her hands above her head. She wore a pair of running pants and a baggy sweatshirt.

"What is this?"

"It's my workout gear."

"For what?"

"You know for what. I joined a gym. I went there tonight after work. Have you done with the whole jealous boyfriend routine? It's a bit much for what we've got going on, Pike."

"You don't need to be working out."

"This isn't about you. It's about me. If I want to lose weight I will."

Pike released her hands, sliding his hands down her arms to cup her breasts. "You've been like this for as long as I've known you. You don't need to lose weight for me. You've got my attention."

"I'm tired, and I smell." She pushed him away and made her way toward the spare room.

"This isn't over, Mary."

She didn't look back. Closing the door in the spare bedroom, she let out a breath. Across the room she saw her reflection staring back at her. She looked tired, and her cheeks were flushed. "Forget about it."

Her body wanted him.

She went to the bathroom, removing the workout clothes from her body. Tugging off the sports bra, she rubbed her breasts. They were aching from being confined in the bra. "God, I hate this."

Turning on the shower she climbed inside, groaning the instant the water washed over her. She was in heaven at washing off the day's sweat and grime from her body. Things were different now with Mac. He knew she was screwing with Pike even if she refused to let her heart get involved. Their friendship was strained. She didn't know if she could trust him.

What made it harder for her was knowing Pike's involvement in her life.

He'd paid for her to work at the diner. When she thought he didn't pay attention to her, he'd been in the background taking care of her.

"I told you, your ass is back in my room."

Mary screamed. He picked her up over his shoulder. She grabbed hold of his leather jacket as he turned off the water, carrying her away.

"Are you completely insane?" she asked.

He didn't stop, just carried her through to his bedroom. "We've got a deal."

"I want a shower."

"You were in the spare bedroom." He placed her in the shower in his room, turning the water on. She squealed as the water was freezing hitting her skin.

"You're such an asshole." Turning her head to the side, she finally saw his black eye. "What happened?" she asked, reaching out to touch his face.

Pike didn't say anything, removing his leather jacket.

"I want to shower alone."

"I care about my environment, and showering together saves energy."

She rolled her eyes. Facing the shower, she closed her eyes enjoying the warmth of the water.

"I want you to stop going to the gym."

"I paid for a year's subscription. This is about me, Pike. I promised myself I'd do this."

"I'll pay you back."

Letting out a sigh, she glanced over at him. He was butt ass naked. She averted her gaze, looking at the tiled wall instead. "I don't want or need your money."

He stepped into the shower stall, his large body making the space incredibly small. His hands went on either side of the wall, trapping her in.

"I want you to quit."

Releasing a growl, she turned to face him. "Not everything is about you, okay? This is something I've wanted for a long time. Do you know what it's like to be called such horrible shit?" She slapped her hand against his chest. "I've been called fat all my life, by parents who should have cared about me, customers, peers, you name it, they've said it. I'm tired of it. This is a change I want to make."

He pressed her against the wall. "You think you need to change?"

"Why are you with me, Pike? You're not a one woman man. There has to be variety for the good old Pike." She slapped his shoulder again, wishing he'd back up.

"I've changed."

She laughed. "Please, I bet you're fucking as much as you used to. God, I can't believe I even slept with you without a condom."

"I'm clean. You're the first woman I've ever fucked without a condom. You're the only woman I fucking want." She snorted. There was no way she could believe him. "I've wanted you a long time, Mary. I couldn't have you. You weren't ready for me. You think Duke's a problem, you've seen nothing yet." He gripped her chin forcing her to look at him. "I want to kill Mac for being near you. I want to torch that fucking diner so you don't have a choice but to ride on the back of my bike. You want truth? I'll give you bastard truth. I've not fucked another woman since you. I took that bitch to the diner, but I've not touched anyone. The only woman I think about is you. The only woman I get hard for, is you."

He bent down, staring into her eyes.

"I'm used to fucking everything. The moment I was inside you, taking what was mine all along, I got scared."

"Pike doesn't get scared."

"I do. You've always been there. After what your parents put you through it's a miracle you were still sane. They were horrible bastards, and all you've got to do is say the word and they're dead."

She shook her head. "Stop, Pike."

He was confusing her.

"I fucked up. You don't trust me, and I get that. I've got to earn back the trust I lost. What I'm asking from you is give me a chance."

"I can't."

He signed. "You think you're fat?"

"I'm not exactly skinny."

Pike released her face to stroke down her cheek going to the pulse at the side of her neck. "I don't see a fat woman. I see *my* woman. Your body is full, ripe." He stroked over her pulse before he moved his hand down to cup her breast. "These tits, they're in my dreams all the time. I think about them bouncing in front of me as I ride you hard. Your nipples are so large, and they're always ready for my lips." He moved his hand to her waist. "You can take everything that I give you, fucking you hard without fear of breaking you."

He landed on her pussy, sliding his fingers through her slit. She gripped his arms to keep her steady. His arms were covered in ink. The club insignia decorated his chest, and she couldn't help but look at it.

"You know what I want from you."

"No, I don't."

"I want you as my old lady."

She shook her head. "Goddamn it. Why are you doing this to me?"

"I'm being open with you."

"This isn't you."

"You've got no idea who I really am. You only know what I've been before. That's not who I really am."

He took his fingers from her pussy, sucking them inside his mouth.

Heat flooded her body at the look of rapture on his face. "You taste so damn good, um, I need more."

She glanced down looking at his cock. He was long and thick. Sinking to her knees, Mary couldn't look at Pike. He was opening up in ways she'd always dreamed about.

No, I won't let him get to me like this. It's unfair.

"Mary?"

"Pleasure, right?"

"I'm opening up to you."

"I don't want to hear it." Wrapping her fingers around his cock, she cupped his balls. The tip was leaking his pre-cum, and she swiped her tongue over it, licking it up. She swallowed his taste down, listening to him groan. Sucking the mushroomed head into her mouth, she flicked her tongue repeatedly over the little slit, tasting more and more of his pre-cum. He was salty and musky.

"If you're going to suck my cock then you're going to do it properly."

She pulled away from his shaft to stare up at him. Her pussy grew slick as he wrapped her hair around his fist. Mary gasped as he tugged on her and she didn't have a choice but to follow him. His other hand went to his cock, running two fingers up and down the shaft.

"You want this?"

Nodding her head, she licked her lips. Over the past couple of weeks she'd noticed he couldn't stand to see her licking her lips. It drove him crazy with arousal.

"Say it. I want to hear it."

"I want to suck your cock, Pike."

He placed the tip to her lips, running it along her bottom then her top lip before pressing into her mouth. She sucked him inside. Pike gripped her hair stopping her from taking more of him inside.

"I'm the one controlling this show, baby."

She stared up his body as he began to thrust his hips into her waiting mouth.

"Fuck, beautiful. You don't have a clue how damn amazing you look with my cock in your mouth."

Mary couldn't look away. He cupped her cheek, caressing over his shaft while she sucked him inside.

The hold in her hair tightened, and he started to feed her more and more of his cock.

"Yeah, that's it, take it all, swallow it."

Moaning, she closed her eyes, loving the feel of his cock in her mouth, the taste of him on her tongue. Each new sensation heightened her own arousal to the point of no return. Slipping her hand between her thighs, she started to touch her clit.

"You're fingering your little pussy, aren't you?" She hummed her response. "Play with your clit." He pumped his dick into her mouth, and Mary sucked every inch of him. Pike withdrew when he hit the back of her throat. She didn't choke, and Pike seemed to know exactly what to do to heighten her own arousal. "When I get you in bed I'm going to fuck you. I'm going to slam every inch of my dick in that pretty pussy, and then I'm going to claim your ass." He groaned. The thrusting of his cock increased into her mouth, and she accepted him, loving the pleasure, the power she held over him.

Pinching her clit like Pike did to her, Mary splintered apart, taking more of his cock into her mouth. Her body ached from the exercise she'd done, yet Pike brought a need so desperate she couldn't deny him.

"I'm going to come," he said.

She was ready for him. Mary was shocked as at the final moment, he pulled out and started spraying his seed onto her chest. He turned the shower off so it didn't wash away either.

Once it was over, she let out a breath.

"Now that is a sight I'm never going to forget." He went down to his knees, going in front of her. "This, it's just the beginning with us, Mary. You can shut me out and pretend we're nothing, and that's fine. It's not going to stop how I feel about you. I'm going to be your man, and you're going to be my old lady."

"My old man?" she asked, smirking.

He tilted her head back. "Yours in everything."

****

Pike woke up the following morning. Turning over he saw the bed was indeed empty. He rarely got the chance to see her asleep in his bed. Letting out a curse, he climbed out of bed, walking toward the kitchen.

He heard music playing in the kitchen and caught the scent of fresh baking.

Completely naked, he entered the kitchen and came to a stop when he saw Duke with six of the guys from the club. Mary wore a pair of jeans and a red shirt that hung off her body.

"Fuck, Pike, clear that shit up," Daisy said, pointing at his junk hanging out.

All of the men turned toward him, chuckling at his naked state. He could do one of two things, either turn and run, or take it all in his stride and show the men he wasn't afraid.

Stepping into the room, he moved toward Mary. Someone slapped him on the ass, and he turned to glare. The men were all in fits of laughter.

"I'll find out who that was and get payback."

Mary was stirring some batter in a bowl as he wrapped his arm around her waist.

"I missed you," he said.

"Someone had to answer the door when they were up. I don't like sleeping late." He'd spent a great deal of last night fucking her, and this was what he got for it, the cold shoulder.

He touched her cheek, turning her to face him. Pressing his lips to hers, he pushed his advantage by slipping his tongue into her mouth. With the men in the room, he slid his hand up to cup her breast.

"Shit, Pike, surely you could have taken the time to put on some pants. My eyeballs are grossed out," Holly said, coming back into the room.

Duke lost all of his happiness. "Put your fucking pants on, man."

"For fuck's sake. You're the ones who've invaded my home and you're telling me to put on pants."

Mary pulled out of his arms, seeing her little slip up in allowing him to kiss her.

Don't worry, baby. I'm not backing down.

"What's going on?" he asked, taking a seat beside Mary.

"Ew, you better clean that chair," Mary said, beating madly at the mixture in her bowl. Glancing at her chest, Pike smirked. Her nipples were rock hard. His little cook wasn't as unaffected by him as she'd like him to believe.

"Bonfire tonight, brother," Daisy said, speaking up.

"Club meeting, it's important."

"You're doing house calls now?" Pike took a sip of Mary's coffee. Holly was working around his kitchen with his woman. Both of them looked at home in the space.

"I was bringing Holly," Duke said.

"It's Saturday, and we've been planning on a big bake off for some time. With her leg all better, we're getting back into the swing of things." Holly bumped her hip against Mary's.

"I couldn't miss the chance to see you all settled down," Daisy said.

"He's not," Mary said, staring at him. "We're not a thing." She gestured between the two of them.

The men went eerily silent. Clenching his teeth together, he watched Mary turn her back on the room. Staring at his friends, his brothers, he shook his head.

"It's church tonight," Duke said. "We've got some things to discuss."

"I'll be there."

Duke rounded the counter going to Holly and drawing her close. "Be careful and call me when you need a ride."

The couple kissed. "Where's Raoul?" Pike asked.

"Who knows? He's been away a couple of days," Pie said.

"Remember, party tonight. I expect you there," Duke said.

He watched them leave. The Trojan insignia was on all of their leather jackets. His own was hung up in his bedroom.

"Hols, leave me alone with Mary for a moment." He spun around to face the two women.

Holly slapped a hand across her eyes. "Too much, Pike. Seriously, would a pair of pants have killed you?"

"I didn't know anyone was coming." Holly walked out of the kitchen, leaving him alone with Mary. "You're coming to the bonfire tonight."

"I'm not."

"You're coming, and don't even think to argue with me." He closed the distance between them, trapping her against the wall to stop her from talking. "I suggest you keep that pretty little mouth closed. You're coming to the bonfire, and when the men are here, you're mine. You're my woman."

"This is just sex."

"That's where you're wrong." He kissed her neck, breathing in her lovely scent. Groaning, he gripped her hip tightly. "When are you going to give me a chance?"

She stayed silent, still in his arms.

"I fucked up, but you're here in my life."

"I can't do this, Pike."

"We're going to do it soon."

"You hurt me. You just expect me to sit down and be this submissive little woman you can do whatever the hell you want to?"

"I'm not going to hurt you."

She spun around to face him. "You already have. I'm having sex with you. What more do you want?"

Pressing his hand over her heart, Pike stared into her eyes. "I want this."

"No, you can't have that. It's not fair for you to press this on me." He watched her swallow, and her eyes glistened with unshed tears. "I've got stuff to do."

"Come to the bonfire with me. I'll prove to you I'm different."

She bit her lip, a very tempting bottom lip.

"Okay, I'll come."

"Holly will be there with you."

"Fine. I said I'll be there. I'm making cakes for the event anyway."

He pressed a kiss to her lips.

"I'll go and get dressed."

Leaving the room, he ran fingers through his hair as he made his way toward the room. He passed Holly who kept her gaze on his face.

When he passed her, Pike stopped. "Will she ever forgive me?"

Glancing over his shoulder he saw Holly had stopped.

"Do you love her?" she asked.

"With all of my heart." His answer was honest.

"Does she know that?"

"No."

"You hurt her real bad. She doesn't trust you. You've got to fight past her walls. They're up. I've seen the way she is with you. She's scared to let go and love you again."

"Again?"

"Come on, Pike, you know Mary has always been in love with you. You're her knight in shining armor." Holly's arms were crossed over her chest. "Do you really think it was sheer bad luck that she was a virgin that night?"

He fisted his hands, watching her.

"Mary, she always envisioned something romantic, a time to remember when she gave herself to you. She's never been loved by a man. Her parents hated her, and you're the only man who ever showed he cared." Holly shrugged her shoulders, tears leaking from her eyes. "I know it's fucked up, but she wants everything with you."

"I want to give her everything. She's holding back on me."

"She's screwing you."

"But I'm not getting anything else from her."

Holly sighed. "Then don't give up. Mary's used to people walking away. I love her. I've never walked away, but I'm not you." She touched his arm. "You'll win her back if you really want to." With that Holly walked away from him.

Going to his room, he went to the closet grabbing out his clothes. He changed quickly, sliding on his jacket. Going into the bathroom, he stared at his reflection.

"Mary, I've fucked up the whole of my life. I've made bad decisions, and I've lived with them. There's nothing I can do to change the shit I've done." He let out a sigh, pulling the small box from his jacket. "I hurt you, and for that no words will ever begin to tell you how sorry I am." He faced himself lifting the box toward the mirror. "I can't live without you. I love you more than anything. I've loved you for a long time, longer than I fucking should have. I'm going to spend the rest of my life making up for the fact I made us wait. I'll show you love, laughter, and pleasure you didn't think was possible. Will you do me the honor of becoming my wife?"

He smiled at his reflection, and for the first time in over twenty years, Pike started to cry. Her answer was the most important in all of his life. The only time he'd ever wanted to get a yes. Wiping away the tears, he pocketed the ring. She wasn't ready for a marriage proposal. With the way she treated him, which he deserved, he doubted she'd ever be ready.

****

"What the fuck is all of this about?" Diaz asked, handing over the four pieces of information.

Raoul stared at the details seeing the men were lowlifes with records.

"I've got business to handle."

"This club business with these four assholes?" Diaz asked, pointing at the papers.

"No, this is personal."

"You know that costs money. I don't do shit for free."

Raoul pulled the two grand fee that Diaz would charge. It was a lot of money, but he'd not been spending any of his share for the last few years. He had more than enough to pay for this information.

"Fuck, man, what did these bastards do?" Diaz pocketed the money.

"They thought it was okay for them to force a woman." Zoe's frightened face entered his mind.

"You know this costs information and a clean-up."

"I don't need you to do the killing. I can handle these four dickless wonders. Take me to the locations. I'll take them out and then you and your crew can clean it up."

"This is personal biz. No bad shit will come between me and the Trojans."

"Good, because if it does, I'll kill you, Diaz. This is personal. Not to do with the club."

"It explains the lack of marks."

Raoul wasn't wearing his leather cut. "Take me to the first one. I've got a bonfire to be at tonight." It was probably going to be the last day that he was a Trojan member. He'd make the most of it by taking these four scumbags off the street.

Chapter Nine

"Hello, ladies," Russ said, climbing out of his car. Sheila, Holly's mother, climbed out the other side. Mary smiled at Holly's parents. Russ and Sheila hugged her close before they embraced their daughter. Mary walked back into the kitchen to pick up the first foil-wrapped chicken pasta. She and Holly had been cooking and baking up a storm.

"It has been too long since we've had a bonfire. This will be my first one in a couple of years," Sheila said.

Glancing over at the older couple, Mary's heart went out to Sheila. Russ stared at his wife with guilt clear in his eyes. Several years back Sheila had been attacked by the enemy of the club, losing her child in the process. From what Holly told her, Russ had then cheated on her, and their relationship had been strained for a while. Sheila pulled away from the club and from Russ, being his old lady in name only, nothing else. It was a sad situation that didn't help the couple's relationship.

"It's going to be fun," Holly said.

Holly had told her tonight was the night they were going to announce her pregnancy to the club. It was going to be a big night for all of them.

Mary packaged up the meatloaf as everyone started to pack everything away. Russ stood beside her, helping her.

"So, are you going to be at the clubhouse tonight?" he asked.

"Yeah, Pike wants me to go." Her hands started to shake as she packaged up the meat. This was the last thing she wanted.

"Are you okay?"

Glancing over at Russ, Mary let out a sigh. Holly and Sheila were organizing the back of the truck to take the food.

"I don't know."

"You've not had the best start in life, I know that. It's been pretty shit with your folks. Mary, I consider you one of my girls. You've been Holly's friend for as long as I can remember. Shit, I recall you both running around the clubhouse causing pranks. I gave you both a little too much leeway in the club." Russ gripped the back of his neck. "As far as I'm concerned, you're my daughter, and because of that, you can come to me about anything."

Tears filled her eyes. It was one of the nicest things ever said to her.

"Thank you." She wrapped her arms around Russ, hugging him close.

"Tell me what's bothering you?" he asked.

"I'm—I'm not used to really telling anyone about my feelings or how upset I am about shit." She sucked in her breath, wishing for some easy way to say the words.

"Pike is an asshole. He's played more than any brother in the club. The bastard is a machine in bed and out of it." Russ cupped her cheek. "But he's also a good man. I know what he's done to take care of you. Not many men would do that unless you were fucking him. I'm not talking about now, I'm talking about before. He took care of you, made sure you had a job, and he didn't need to do either. I'm not going to tell you to give in too quickly."

"I've loved him for a long time," she said, admitting the truth. "He hurt me, and I'm scared that I'm going to get hurt again, and I don't want to."

Russ tutted. "Honey, life is pain. Love, hate, it's all going to get you hurt. Sheila, she's my old lady, the woman I love more than anything. It didn't stop me from

SAM CRESCENT

hurting her. I paid for my sins and it has taken me a long time to earn her forgiveness, but I've got it. Pike, he fucked up. Do you think he's going to fuck up again, or do you think he's finally gotten the message?"

"I don't know." She stared down at her locked fingers, unable to find any truth in her life anymore.

"Pike wants you at the bonfire. You're living in his house, and I'd say from the kitchen, Pike's been there when you didn't even fucking realize he was. Give him a chance, Mary. The man, he may surprise you."

Smiling, she nodded. "Okay."

"When you're with him, though, it doesn't mean you have to stop making him earn it. Men love a challenge."

She chuckled, following him out with the last of the food.

"Are you two driving up with us?" Russ asked.

"Yeah. I'm just going to grab my coat."

Mary walked back inside and grabbed her jacket. Glancing around the room, she let out a sigh. Maybe it was time to give a little for Pike. She didn't know what to think. He'd given her a job for Mac, and then there was the kitchen.

"Are you okay?"

"Yeah, I will be. I think."

"The club, it's not all bad." Holly placed her arm over Mary's shoulders. "I mean, yeah, it's scary when they go on runs and stuff. Duke, he's a good man, and he makes sure the men are good."

"It's not the club that scares me, Hols."

"What is it?"

Shaking her head, Mary put her jacket on. It was late February and still cold outside.

"I've loved Pike a long time. Yeah, it was a stupid girl crush, but it became more." Placing a hand on her

127

stomach, Mary pressed her lips together unsure what to say next.

"Just say it, Mary. You'll feel better."

"I'm scared to love him. He hurt me, and I didn't think I'd ever get over it. I'm changing who I am, and he's asking me to be this person I always wanted to be." She stopped to press a hand over her heart. "Damn, I'm scared."

"When you're in love with someone, it's scary. It's not going to change no matter how much you want it to." Holly pulled her in for a hug. "Do you remember after the shit with Raoul? We both agreed we'd not get stuck down by men or become part of the club either as a whore or an old lady."

Mary laughed. They'd spent the whole summer by the lake when they weren't working. Not many people would touch them as Holly was club royalty.

"Pike was always there at the lake keeping everyone back, Mary. He's the one who found our apartment and paid the bulk of our rent."

"What?"

"On our incomes, we couldn't afford that place. It was perfect, two bathrooms, a large kitchen. Yeah, it was small and modest, but it was a dream. We couldn't afford it. Duke told me. Pike has been taking care of you a long time, honey." Holly cupped her face. "I think you've got a bad case of denial with Pike. Sometimes you've got to take a chance."

"Take a chance?"

"Come on, Mary. Ever since you've been living here I've seen a difference in you. You're happy, you're always smiling, and you're fun. This is who you were supposed to be. Give it a shot, for yourself."

"And if I get my heart broken?"

"We'll camp out at my place, which also happens to be Duke's place. I'm consoling my heartbroken friend so he's not getting any." Holly raised her hand in the air. "Duke's the head of the club. Duke's not getting laid by his woman because of her friend, one of his men broke her friend's heart, Pike's gets his ass thoroughly kicked, hell yeah." Holly raised her hands in the air, crying out in joy. "I'll be there for you like I've always been. We're best friends, and I love you."

Holding onto Holly, Mary hugged her tighter than ever before. In her whole world the one person she'd always been able to trust was Holly.

Take a chance. Live a little.
****

Pike sat at his place at the table. The doors were closed, giving the club privacy. Music could be heard in the background as the bonfire started up. Russ sat at the opposite end of the table.

"We've got another run in three weeks. We're going straight to Vegas, doing the drop with Ned Walker. He's then dealing with the shit from there."

"What's going on with The Skulls?" Russ asked. "We don't want to be stepping on anyone's toes."

"We've got no beef with The Skulls. I told you, they're backing out, and anything that happens from Vegas onwards is not our concern. We're not even passing close to Fort Wills or Piston County. I want the club to stay clear of all that mess. You got personal preferences, tell me now and I'll vote your asses out of the club." Duke looked at each man waiting for them to speak up.

"Fuck, no. Chaos Bleeds and The Skulls are going to get themselves killed one of these days. I like my life, and I'm going to keep on living it," Daisy said.

All the men joined in agreement. The other two MCs were bad news. They'd had a lot of casualties over the past few years. A lot of heat and a lot of shit that moving coke and guns didn't need. Pike respected both Devil and Tiny for staying out of shit. It's what a good president of a club did.

"We're not all going on this run," Duke said, leaning forward. "I need several men to stay back to keep an eye on the club and the women."

Pike held his hand up. "I'll stay behind. Daisy can wear the VP patch for the trip."

"You got a reason for that, brother?" Duke asked.

"Mind's not in the game. I'd be useless. I got to get shit settled here before I even ride with the club."

"Mary?" Russ asked.

"Yeah. I'm going to be making her my old lady. You got a problem with that?" Pike directed his question at the whole table.

"Does she know, yet?"

"No, but she will."

"You claiming her tonight?" Duke asked. "It'll give her better protection."

"I'll need several of the club brothers close to witness it."

"You need a minimum of seven to do this," Duke said.

"I don't want to see," Russ said, shaking his head. "It's nothing personal. I know women can be stubborn. Mary, she's like a daughter to me."

"When it's done, I'll tell her, Russ. I'm not going to hurt her again."

"You better not or I'm going to hurt you."

Pike nodded.

"I'll be there. I witness it, I see it, the ruling stands that Mary is an old lady, protected by the club. I'll talk to Holly. Let her know not to say anything."

"You're putting a lot of pressure on the friendship," Russ said.

"I'm doing what's best for the woman I love and the club. She'll understand." Duke rubbed his hands. "The next order of business." Pike watched as Duke looked at Raoul.

"Fuck, man, you're going to do this now?"

"The next order of business. I'm going to apologize to you, Raoul."

"Wait, what?"

"I was going to request to vote you out. Instead, I'm apologizing. The shit that happened with you and Holly, it should have stayed in the past. Instead, I brought it to the front and shouldn't have. For that, it's my fault, and I apologize. I will not be voting you out."

Duke reached over to shake Raoul's hand.

Pike covered his smirk behind his hand as did all the brothers. Raoul looked totally shocked and blown away by Duke's apology.

"Okay, moving on. Final piece of news. Holly's announcing that she's pregnant tonight to the whole of the club. This is why I need at least one of you to stay behind to keep an eye on her. I'd do it myself, but I can't. Keep an eye on her, make sure she takes her meds, and we'll be fine."

Duke slammed the gavel down bringing a close to the business.

"I'm going to be a granddaddy?" Russ asked.

"Yes, act surprised when Holly tells you." Duke got to his feet, taking congratulations from the men. Pike shook his hand before heading out of the clubhouse.

Several of the club whores were waiting for the men to leave church. Baby rushed toward him.

"How about I show you how awesome I can be?" she asked. "I'll suck your cock and have you begging for more?"

Mary chose that moment to walk out of the kitchen with Holly beside her.

Baby wore a mini skirt that showed the whole of her ass along with the tiny g-string she wore.

"I'm taken, Baby." He pushed her off him handing her toward Daisy. Pike stepped toward Mary, aware of the gazes of everyone in the room. Without waiting for her permission, he sank his fingers into her hair, tugging her close. Slamming his lips on hers, he held her tightly to him, rubbing his cock against her stomach. She gripped his arms, not pushing him away. Breaking from the kiss he stared into her eyes. "No one but you."

She nodded. "I take it your meeting has finished?"

"Yeah, the food ready?" he asked.

"Yes."

"I'm going to make my announcement." Holly smiled at the two of them, heading toward Duke.

"Let's get out of here." Pike urged her through the door toward the kitchen.

"You don't want to stick around to hear?"

"I know she's pregnant. I want you all to myself until the party really gets in full swing." He grabbed both of their jackets, putting hers on her before taking her outside to the cold.

"Holly told me what happens in church stays in church?" Mary said.

He closed the door as cheers started to erupt. "It does. I'll tell you whatever you need to know. Club business is not your business."

SAM CRESCENT

"It's okay. I, erm, I don't want to know anything illegal or that can get me into trouble." She turned to smile at him. He watched her tuck some hair behind her ear. Pike gripped her arm. "What?"

Pike locked their fingers together, holding her hand. "I want to hold you."

"Are you being a romantic?" she asked. Her cheeks were a lovely shade of red.

"I'm trying to be."

There was something different about her. She wasn't ignoring him or pulling away. In fact, she reminded him of the Mary she used to be before he hurt her.

"It makes a change. You trying to be romantic."

"I've not had a lot of practice at it. The club whores don't exactly make you work for it."

The smile died on her lips.

"No, I guess not."

"I'm not going to screw with them."

"I remember you said that you'd not been with anyone else since me."

"I've not. I'm not lying to you." They walked out the back of the clubhouse toward the open fields. He loved the back of the clubhouse. It was like a paradise when so much bad shit happened in the club. They'd made a lot of decisions to live or die in that one room. Duke was a good president, one of the best. "I'm not going to lie to you, Mary. I've had a lot of pussy, a lot more than even Duke's ever had. None of them, they're not you." He stopped to press her up against the nearest tree.

"I believe you." She gave him a smile.

"You're not going to argue with me over this?" he asked, touching her cheek.

"I'm going to give us a chance." Her gaze went to his chest. "I'm scared to trust you."

"That's all my fault. I was the one who put those doubts inside that head."

"Why did you do it, Pike? Why couldn't you leave me alone or not call? Why did you have to break my heart and say those mean things?" Tears were streaming out of her eyes. Seeing her crying hurt him more than anything he'd ever realized.

"I was scared." He stopped to clear his throat. A lump formed in his throat, and he gritted his teeth as he wanted to cry along with her. "You've always been my weakness, Mary. You don't know how much of a weakness you've been." He tilted her head back to stare into her eyes. "Being near you, inside you, it was better than I imagined. I didn't know what happened to me. All I saw was me hurting you. I thought I couldn't give you what you deserved, love, commitment, being faithful. After I did what I did, I realized what a big fucking mistake I made. I tried to come and see you, to make amends. You were always busy working. I was a coward, Mary."

He touched her cheek, stroking over her pale flesh. There were times he couldn't believe she was in his arms.

"Seeing you hurt with your leg, I'd never been so damned scared in the whole of my life. I had to do something. I'll always be there for you, Mary. I'm begging you for your forgiveness for what I did."

"You're begging?"

He dropped to his knees in front of her, pressing his face against her stomach. "You've won, baby. Do you know what it was like to wake up every morning but you not be there? You wouldn't let me kiss you, and every chance you got, you denied we were together. You've cut

SAM CRESCENT

me out of your life in all the ways that mattered." He snorted. "You wouldn't even look at me anymore. Your eyes would always look over my shoulder or find something else to look at. I've never been so desperate."

"I forgive you," she said. She wiped at her tears, stroking her fingers through his hair. "I forgive you, but don't hurt me again." Picking her up in his arms, Mary wrapped her legs around his waist.

"I won't. I promise."

Claiming her lips, Pike only had one thing left to do, take her in front of his brothers.

Chapter Ten

The bonfire was fun. Mary had been to several parties over the years with Holly. Neither of them had parties late at night with the club. This was all new to her, old ladies and club whores, the men. She glanced toward the main forecourt of the compound to see Russ and Sheila dancing together. The couple was happy. The news of Holly's pregnancy brought joy to the whole of the club.

The happy couple was sitting at the table with her and Pike.

"If I'd known my baby would bring them together I'd have gotten pregnant sooner," Holly said.

Her friend leaned against Duke, who was drinking a beer. Matthew was at the party earlier but had been sent home with a babysitter.

"They're going to be grandparents. You'll get a lot of free child care," Mary said.

"Yeah, I will."

"It'll give us plenty of time to make another one."

Holly slapped Duke on the arm. "Stop it. I want to get this one over and done with first."

Mary watched as Duke placed his hand on Holly's stomach. "Everything is going to be fine." Duke kissed her neck, sucking on her flesh.

"Stop it, we have guests."

"So? Pike can do whatever he wants to Mary." Duke tilted his beer in their direction.

Chuckling, Mary leaned against Pike. His hand rested on her thigh. She had her leg out in front of her on the bench. Her leg was all healed up, but the doctor had warned her that at times it'd feel stiff. Pike's gentle strokes were helping to ease out the stiffness and also turning her on.

"It's getting really cold," Holly said.

"There's a small group of guys inside. No other women," Duke said, staring at Pike.

"What's the matter?" Mary asked, glancing between both men.

"Nothing. I just thought now would be a good time to take the party inside."

"Duke?" Holly asked. The happy couple shared a look. "Yes. I think it would be a good time to take this inside."

She watched the couple stand up, heading toward the clubhouse. Duke said something to Russ as he passed.

"What's going on?" Mary asked, confused.

"Nothing. Come on. I'm freezing my ass off. I'm sure it's why your leg is giving you some problems."

"How did you know?" she asked.

"I called your doctor when I saw you a few nights ago rubbing your leg when we were watching a movie. I figured that's why you're leg was out like it was." Pike got to his feet helping her up. "Hold onto me."

She held onto him as they walked toward the clubhouse. Moving around helped ease out the stiffness of her leg. "You're probably right, it's the cold."

"My brave little woman." They entered the clubhouse, and Pike picked her up over his shoulder.

"What are you doing, Pike? Put me down." She slapped his ass, giggling as he swatted her own.

He placed her on the pool table in the center of the room. She glanced around the room to see Daisy, Raoul, Pie, Duke, and Holly, along with a few men. None of them paid her any attention. The lighting of the room was turned down, creating a sensual scene in the room. The music was slow. Her body warmed under Pike's gaze.

"What's going on?" she asked.

His fingers rubbed her leg, making her moan in pleasure at the attention he devoted to her.

"Do you trust me?" he asked.

"What?" His hand cupped her against her jeans. "Pike?"

"We've got a rule at the club, Mary. It's a strict one, and I can't let you leave this room until after I take you."

"Take me?" Glancing around the room she noticed Holly was making out with Duke. The two were not looking toward them. The men, they were watching the scene.

"You're going to be my old lady."

"No, I'm not. I'm not ready for that." Mary gripped his arm, pushing him away. He released her immediately.

"I want you, Mary."

"I just offered you my forgiveness for treating me like a whore when I gave you my virginity. You made my first time one of the worst experiences in the world, and now you want to claim me as an old lady. Is this some kind of an orgy?" she asked. She hadn't let him go.

"It's not an orgy. This is going to make sure you're protected."

"The only reason I'm not protected is because of the club." Her heart was racing. The thought of Pike screwing her turned her on, even with the men in the room. The thought of another touching her, doused any kind of arousal.

"I can't do this. Is this what you were going to do? Fuck me on the table for others to see?"

She saw the truth in his eyes.

"You hoped I'd want you too damned much not to give in." She jumped off the pool table, wincing at the pain going up her leg. Pike tried to help her. She pushed him away. "No, I don't want you to touch me."

"Mary?" Holly said.

She turned on her friend. "Is this what you did? Fucked them all to be protected?"

Duke rose to his feet.

"Mary, please, this is what the club—"

"No, I'm not doing this." She stepped away from Pike. "I'm not doing any of this." She made her way toward the door without looking back.

"This is what the old ladies do, Mary," Pike said.

Turning back to look at him, Mary let him see the whole truth of the pain he'd caused. "It's a good job I never wanted to be an old lady." Opening the door, she found Russ stood guarding the door from the outside.

It was all planned. Duke suggesting they go inside, him talking to Russ.

"Mary?"

"No, I can't deal with this now. This is too much." She shoved her way passed, moving out of the clubhouse. They all fucked each other while watching. No, she couldn't do that. When Pike had her up against the tree, she'd truly thought he was being caring, loving, even. It was all a mistake. This was too much to take in right now. What kind of club fucked women like that? It was wrong.

Walking the streets toward town, Mary found herself knocking on Mac's door. He was the only person she could think of to go to. It was late, it was cold, and she didn't want to go anywhere else.

Seconds later Mac opened the door. He was wearing a pair of jeans with a white shirt.

"Mary, shit, are you okay?" he asked.

"I know this is a lot to ask. Could I come in?"

"Sure." He opened the door wider to allow her inside. "You know I'm always happy to have you at my place." He closed the door behind her.

"Do you want to tell me what's going on?" he asked.

Did she? The club business had to stay part of the club.

"I've had an argument with Pike. I don't have an apartment anymore. You're the only one I could think to come to."

"What about Holly?"

"Yeah, I can't go to her right now."

She bit her lip, taking a seat on his sofa. His apartment was surprisingly tidy, a complete contrast to his office. She'd spent a great deal of time fixing his office.

"Look, Pike, he cares about you. You can't tell me what's going on, and I'm guessing that's club shit. You can stay here however long you want."

"I don't want to sleep with you. Our relationship is never going to change," she said.

"Whoa, I'm not going to make demands. I think we both know Pike has always been the one, not me."

Tears filled her eyes as she thought about what just happened. She'd not really let him explain.

"I, erm, I don't know what to do. I'm so confused right now. They just sprang it on me without giving me the chance to think things through."

Mac sat beside her, tugging her close. "It's okay. I'll be here when you need me. I like being your friend. I care about you, and that's not going to change."

Resting her head against his chest, Mary let the tears fall.

She was in love with Pike. Talking to him against the tree, she hadn't lied to him. She did forgive him.

Hating him had never been something she could do. What she didn't know was if she could take that next step with him.

****

"She's not answering her cell and neither are her parents at the trailer. I'm telling you, her parents would be the last place she'd go," Holly said.

Pike stood inside Duke's home, trying to think of what to do next. He'd not followed her out of the clubhouse, which had been the biggest mistake he'd made.

"I told you he needed to tell her, Duke. I didn't exactly handle it well. Their history, what made you think Mary would handle it any better?" Holly threw her phone against the wall. Her anger had peaked since Mary stormed out of the clubhouse. Russ hadn't been too impressed either.

"You need to calm down, Holly," Duke said, moving behind his wife, holding her close.

"Calm down? Calm down? I just had my best friend walk out on me looking at me like a stranger when all I was trying to do was help her. God, she's in love with you, Pike. Always has been and you've got to find ways of screwing it up." Holly's temper was high, her hormones obviously affecting her attitude.

"I love her, Holly. I did what I thought was best."

"Well, you screwed up there." Holly moved toward him. "You better make this right with her."

Duke wrapped his arms around her waist, pulling her back. Pike wouldn't have hurt her. He didn't believe in physically harming a woman.

"Have you considered calling Mac?" Matthew asked, walking into the sitting room. He carried a soda in his hand. Pike hadn't even heard him wake up.

"What?"

"Mac. He's got a place in town above the diner. If she's not going to her folks, she's not here or at home, she'd go to him."

"And you know this how?" Duke asked.

"I listened. Mary likes to talk. They work together, but they're still friends."

"I'm going to head out to the diner," Pike said.

At the door, Holly called his name. Turning toward her he waited. "Please make it right with her," she said.

"I will." He left Duke's house, climbing on his bike as he made his way toward the diner. The town was quiet, and it was late. He'd fucked up, but then he was always fucking up with his woman. Parking his bike, he started banging on Mac's door. Resting his hands on either side of the wall, he waited for Mac to open.

He was rewarded seconds later.

"Please, tell me she's here," he said.

Mac stepped out of the door, closing it behind him. "She's sleeping on the sofa."

"I need to see her. I need to explain."

"You needed to explain to her before you did whatever you did. She's hurting right now."

"She's mine, Mac."

"Cut the crap. We both know she belongs to you. I get it. She's yours. I don't want a woman in my life who is in love with another man. I don't get my kicks like that." Mac ran fingers through his hair. "I care about Mary, but I don't love her. I saw my parents make the diner strong. I figured with Mary as my wife, we'd make it strong, but I don't love her. You need to make it right for her. Give her a day or two to clear her head. When she's ready, I'll let you know where to find her."

"You better not be starting any crap with me," Pike said. He couldn't believe he was going to walk away.

"No crap. We're friends, Pike, or did you forget that in your obsession with this woman? It has always been one favor after another with you. You think I didn't realize you were in love with her. Mary doesn't want me, and I'm not about to press an advantage for a woman I only care about."

"If that's the case, why did you start trying to date her, huh?"

"You told me to, Pike. You told me to show her a good time. You didn't fucking give me a lot of choice. You'd hurt her, and I didn't like seeing her hurt." Mac shook his head. "Go, clear your head. Make a decision about Mary, and when you do, stick to it, and don't let her get away again."

Mac turned around, slamming into his apartment.

Looking up at the apartment building, Pike struggled to turn and leave.

Give her time.

Walking away from that apartment was the hardest thing he ever did.

****

Raoul stared down at the piece of paper in his hand. Diaz had come through for him again. Zoe's address was a small apartment off the college campus. Turning off his bike, Raoul pocketed the address. It was late. The bonfire had sucked big time with Mary running out. That was going to cause some problems for Pike and possibly the club. Zoe had been on his mind ever since he'd saved her a few weeks ago.

"Okay, come on." He entered the apartment building, not liking the lack of security.

He climbed the four flights of steps toward her room. Knocking on the door, Raoul leaned against the opposite wall, waiting. When she didn't answer right away, he knocked again.

This time she answered the door, rubbing at her eyes. "Yes," she said.

She wore the cutest pajamas with cupcakes on them.

"Oh, hi," she said. Her cheeks went red.

"Can I come in?"

"Yeah, sure." She let him inside, and he waited for her to close the door. "I didn't know you knew where I lived."

"I dropped you outside of the building."

"I didn't give you my number though." She wrapped her arms around her body, rubbing the chill. He noticed there was no heating on. "I'm sorry it's cold. I can't afford to heat my apartment throughout the night."

"How the fuck do you stay warm?"

She smiled. "I've got a big fluffy blanket."

"Sorry for interrupting your night."

"You're not. I fell asleep while studying. Believe me, you're not interrupting anything."

"Those guys, I wanted to let you know that you don't have to worry about them anymore." He rubbed the back of his head.

Zoe tensed, tears filling her eyes.

"You don't have to worry about them ever again." He spoke the words softly.

"Are they dead?" she asked.

"I can't tell you that."

"I saw your leather jacket. You're part of an MC, right? Like the ones people are always talking about nowadays?" She took a step back from him.

"I'm not going to hurt you. I'm part of a club in Vale Valley, the Trojans MC. You ever heard of it?"

She chuckled. "No, I've never heard of it. I don't exactly get out much."

"Well, if you ever want to party, I'd love to see you out of the city." He reached behind his back, pulling out a gun.

"You're not going to kill me, are you?"

"No, I'm giving you a gun."

"Why would you do that?" she asked.

"Living in the city. It's dangerous, and if you had a gun, you'd be protected." He handed it to her. Raoul also handed her a card. "I've paid for you to have lessons so you know how to use it."

"I don't think this is a good idea. I'm not exactly—" She held the gun between her fingers and away from her body. "I'm not good at this."

"May I?" he asked, stepping behind her.

"Sure." She sounded breathless as he stepped behind her. He showed her how to hold the gun.

"This will not hurt you. The safety is on." He showed her the safety then placed it back on. "Put it away, but take the lessons." He didn't want her getting hurt.

"Okay, I appreciate this."

He stepped away from her going toward the door. "You can't tell anyone I was here."

"I wouldn't do that."

Raoul glanced back at the woman who'd gotten under his skin. Her bright red hair and startling green eyes would stay with him forever. "You take care, Zoe. Don't let anyone hurt you, and don't fall for any man's shit."

BETRAYAL

Opening the door, Raoul closed it behind him. Part of him hoped it wasn't the last time he saw the woman.

Chapter Eleven

Mary sat on the ground down by the Vale Valley lake a couple of days after the bonfire. She was wrapped up in a jacket, scarf, and gloves as it was still so cold. She'd had a lot of time to think in the last couple of days. At the bonfire, she'd overreacted, leaving before giving Pike a chance to explain. Mac had told her Pike had come looking for her on the night but Mac had demanded he give her time. She hadn't gone to see him yet. For the past couple of days she'd tried to go and see him, but then stopped herself from taking that next step. What did she say to him? She was so embarrassed by her actions.

Resting her hands on her knee she stared at the water. It was so calm, completely the opposite of what was going on inside her head.

"I thought I'd find you here." She looked up to see Pike stepping out of the forest of trees.

She didn't move as he came to crouch beside her.

"What are you doing here?" she asked.

He reached out to take her hand. "You're here. There's nowhere else I'd rather be than beside you."

"I'm so confused right now." She stared at their locked hands. His hands were much larger than her own.

"I know."

"I've tried to make sense of what was happening, but it doesn't kind of compute."

"There's nothing wrong with that, baby. I want to tell you the truth." He pushed several strands of her hair out of the way.

"Okay, tell me."

He sat with his body around her back but so he was facing her. She turned her head to look him in the eye. This conversation wasn't one to have without looking at each other.

"The women are separated in the club into whores and old ladies."

"I know this."

"The whores, they get into the club and are allowed to stay by fucking several members one after the other. We take turns to initiate them."

Tears filled her eyes thinking about Baby, Samantha, all of the women who hung around the club.

"They get tested regularly, and we all practice safe sex. The women we don't know, they don't get a lot of chance to be with the men. They've got to earn their spot."

"So when the women get voted in, what happens?"

"Simple, their job is to fuck. To fuck, clean, do the laundry, stay out of the old ladies' way. They keep the men happy who want them."

"Does Duke use them?"

"Not since he made the decision to take Holly as his old lady. They're there to be used, but it doesn't mean we use them, Mary."

"What about the old ladies?" Mary asked, squeezing his hand.

"I don't know why it came about or why it happened, I only know what it means to me. An old lady, you claim her, fuck her, in front of the club. They watch, and no one is allowed to touch. If the member invites you, she's a whore and club property all the way with no one owner. No one gets invited, it's a union of two people into one. That's what I wanted to happen Saturday night. I don't want to share you with the club." He squeezed her hand a little tighter. "You're mine, and taking you in front of my brothers, they know to keep their hands off you but they also know to protect you. I couldn't stand for another man to touch you, Mary. If it came down to it, old ladies are worth more than any club whore. Pussy, it's available all day, every day. An old lady, she's precious and to be worshipped. The club respects that."

"Does this happen with every MC?"

"I don't know. I only think about the Trojans. I never cared what another club did or do."

"Precious and worshipped?" she said. His words were going around and around in her head.

"Yes."

"Do you even like me?" She stared into his eyes, hoping to spot the truth.

"Mary, I've been in love with you since before I was allowed."

"Wait, what?" Her heart pounded at his confession.

"You were sixteen, so fucking young. You'd walked into the clubhouse to get a soda for you and Holly. I think you were studying, I don't know. I was arguing with one of the club whores. She wanted my dick. I can't even remember what had happened. All I remember is that she walked out of the club and you came up to me, placed your hand on my shoulder and told me that any woman who could walk away from me that easy, didn't deserve my love. You told me that if given the chance, you'd love me until the day you died."

Mary had forgotten all about that. It was the first and only time she'd really put herself out there. At sixteen she'd not really known what the club was all about or what it meant. She'd always been in love with Pike, and it never stopped.

"I was used to your crush, but do you know what I realized?" he asked.

She shook her head. The tears that were in her eyes spilled down her cheeks.

"In all of my years with women, not one had ever told me she loved me and would love me until the day she died. I was brought to my knees by a sixteen-year-old girl. I vowed to protect you. I was never going to touch you, Mary. I'm not into little girls, so don't be thinking about it. I just wanted to preserve that love you had. I never wanted to see you hurt." He cupped her cheek, stroking over the flesh. "I fucked up in so many ways I can't even remember them all. I protected you, but I didn't wait for you. I always believed you'd find someone to love who deserved you. No one ever came along."

"I never wanted anyone, Pike."

"Then I fucked you that night and treated you no better than a whore. Fuck, do you know how much I regret that? I didn't think I could be faithful to you. I didn't believe I had it in me to give you everything you deserve. I was wrong. I can't even look at another woman. There's no one else I want."

He started moving behind her, and Mary gasped as a small box was placed in front of her.

"What is this?"

"I want you to open it."

With shaking fingers she took the box from him and opened it. Inside a beautiful diamond ring glinted back at her. "What is this?"

"I'm asking you to be my future, Mary. I want you to be my wife. I don't need for you to be my old lady if I can have you as my wife. I'll protect you myself."

"You didn't ask," she said, turning to look at him.

"Then this is me asking. I can't promise I'll never fuck up. I will. I'll turn up to dinner late, I'll forget to put the toilet seat down, and I'll even fart at the most inconvenient of times." She dropped her head to chuckle. He cupped her face, making her look back at him. "But I do love you, Mary. I love you more than anyone in the whole world. You're the only woman I've ever wanted to sleep next to. You're the one I want to sink inside each and every night. The one I want to have babies with, wake up on Christmas morning and not care about the world around me. I only want you. I betrayed your trust, but the biggest betrayal was mine. I never wanted your cherry the way I made out, Mary. I loved being the only man to have you, but it was more than that. I'm in love with you. I will be faithful to you." He pressed a kiss to her lips. "Please say yes and give me the opportunity to make you the happiest woman in the world."

"Well, for a guy who doesn't do romance, you sure know how to make me surprised."

He took the ring out of the box, throwing it away. "Say yes." He slid the ring on her finger. It fit perfectly. "I can't take it back now. The box is in the lake, and I'm not getting in there to get it out."

She chuckled. "Then I guess I better say yes."

"Yes?"

"Yes." She couldn't stop smiling as his mouth moved over hers. He held her tighter than she ever recalled him holding her.

"I love you, Mary."

"And I love you." She pulled away a little, doubt filling her thoughts and dimming the happy moment. "I don't know if I'll be able to do that in front of the club, but I get why you do it. I'm so sorry for acting out. In a strange way, it's really sweet of the club, in a very strange, stranger than strange way."

"I don't care. I've got ways of keeping you safe. I only want you, and I mean every word of it." He cupped her cheek, holding her against him.

Mary closed her eyes, wishing for it to never end.

"I love you, Pike. I never stopped loving you even when you were an ass and I wanted to hate you."

"Come on, I think it's time for us to get off this wet ground and get back home. We can talk to the town soon and the club." He helped her off the ground, and she followed him out to his bike. The ring on her finger made her smile brighter than ever before.

****

One month later

"I'm not wearing a penguin suit," Pike said.

"Come on, you'll look totally hot in it." Mary held the suit that she'd just picked up from the dry cleaners. He knew because Sheila had graciously called him to let him know what Mary had planned.

"I look hot in my leathers."

"You can't wear your leathers to church. I agreed on white when we both know you've taken care of that state for me. I'm long past being a virgin." She held the suit out to him.

"Actually, you've still got one hole that you're a virgin in. It counts." He folded his arms over his chest. For the past month, Pike had been making love, and fucking, Mary at every opportunity. He didn't even care if she was working at the diner. He'd march back, take her to the office, fuck her brains out, and leave. Pike had even called her to the club. Who knew engaged men could get so much action? He sure didn't. However, he'd tried to lure her into something he wanted, teasing her ass, trying to get her ready for him to claim her little anus. She wouldn't let him, and he refused to force the issue even though it made her hotter than hell when he pressed a finger inside her.

She couldn't argue when her cunt was slick from the teasing he gave to her ass. No, she couldn't, yet she wouldn't let him go any further.

"You're not going on about that, are you? I'm not a virgin where it counts."

He stepped closer to her, wrapping his arm around her waist. "You get so damned hot when I'm teasing your ass. I know you'd love my cock inside you, Mary. I've seen the kind of books you read. I've read a few pages. I can give you what you want. I'll make all of your fantasies come true."

"Will you wear the suit?" she asked.

"Are you bargaining with me?"

"Will it work?"

"Your ass for a suit?"

"Yes." She went on her toes, smiling at him. "I'm not above using my body when it comes to you."

"Then I'll wear the suit." He took the hanger from her fingers, throwing it across the sofa. Pike lifted Mary up in his arms carrying her back to his bed.

"What are you doing?"

"I'm not going to give you the chance to change your mind." Dropping her to the bed, he lifted the bottom of her dress up, cupping her pussy. "You're thinking dirty thoughts, baby, or you want my dick in this ass as much as I do."

She knelt on the bed as he stroked over her pussy. She was burning his hand with how hot she was. He slipped his fingers behind her panties, running them over her clit.

Mary cried out, and he pushed her dress over her hips. He tore the panties from her body, before grabbing the condom and lubrication from his drawer. Placing them on the bed, he shoved his jeans off his body and started to undress.

"Get naked for me, baby."

He watched her shuffle out of the dress until she was lying on the bed staring up at him. Pike tore into the condom, sliding it over his cock before climbing between her thighs. She opened up to him, moaning as he bumped her clit with his shaft. Sliding down, he pressed into her tight pussy. Slamming inside, he watched her arch off the bed, gripping the sheets with her scream.

"That's it, baby. I'm so deep inside you. Come for me." Flicking his fingers over her pussy, he teased her clit while bumping inside her cunt.

Mary came apart in his arms, squeezing his cock in her need.

In quick movements, he pulled out, flipping her onto her knees. He grabbed the lube, opening it up and spreading a good amount over his condom covered cock. When his cock was slick, he placed the tip of the lube against her ass and started to work the gel over her puckered hole. She was still coming down from her orgasm. Pike used her pleasure to his advantage. Using his fingers, he worked a digit inside her. She was so damned tight.

He worked a second finger into her ass, stretching her wide.

"I'm going to take it slow and easy. I won't hurt you."

Removing his fingers from her ass, he gripped the base of his cock. Pressing the tip to her puckered hole, he took his time, slowly feeding his dick into her ass. She tensed underneath him, and he paused, waiting for her to get used to the size of him.

"You're big, Pike. I think this is a big mistake."

Pike started to tease over her clit, stroking her to life. Her protests soon turned into moans. Within minutes she started to grind back against him.

"I want you to stroke your clit for me."

Her hand disappeared underneath her. He knew the moment she started touching her clit as her ass went tighter than ever before. Slowly, he worked his cock into her ass, and Mary screamed out as he thrust the last inch into her ass.

"It's okay, baby. I've got you. I'm inside."

"You're big."

"I know, but it feels good, right?"

"Yes," she said, breathing out a sigh of relief.

He gripped her hips, waiting for her to get accustomed to his size. When she started thrusting back against him, Pike began to move, feeding his cock in and out of her ass. The lube made it easy for him to thrust into her ass.

Mary started to push back against him. Her arousal increased with each stroke over her clit.

"I wish you can see what I see. Your ass looks so damned good taking my cock."

"Please, Pike, fuck me."

He increased his thrusts, going inside her. They set up a pace, fucking each other harder. Pike held her hips tightly as he slammed into her ass. The tightening of her ass told him she was getting closer to orgasm.

"That's it, baby, come for me. I want to feel this ass tightening."

When Mary cried out moments later in orgasm, Pike picked up his pace, following her into orgasm. For her first time he didn't want to prolong it and make it painful. He filled the condom, collapsing over her back as the pleasure numbed every single one of his senses.

"I can't believe I just did that."

"You're the one that bargained your body for a suit."

Mary giggled, glancing over her shoulder at him. He kissed her cheek, unable to resist the temptation she created.

"Pike?"

"Yeah, baby."

"I was ready for you to fuck my ass without the bargain."

"You little minx."

Chapter Twelve

"The cake is ordered, and the priest has agreed to do the service in April. We're on course for a spring wedding. All we need to do is the final fitting for Holly…" Sheila kept talking, but Mary was no longer listening. They were a month away from her wedding. It was now March, and for the past two months she'd had a blissful life with Pike. A blissful time where she'd been able to think about Pike and the club, and the claiming. The more she thought about it, the less strange it sounded.

This morning though, she'd woken up unable to stop thinking about the claiming he talked about at the club. She knew it meant a great deal to him, yet she'd not given him a chance to talk about it or given him an indication that she wanted to give him what he wanted. He'd been so sweet and thoughtful. She felt like a total bitch for not giving him a chance.

Mary had visited the club and no one treated her any differently, but she knew something was missing. She didn't *need* to do it. Pike wasn't pressuring her.

"Earth to Mary." Sheila ran her hand in front of her face.

Pulling back, Mary smiled. "Sorry, I was lost in my own little thoughts."

"Do you want to talk about it?" Holly asked.

She was sat in Sheila's home arranging the last part of the wedding.

"This, erm, this claiming thing. You know where the men watch. You know what? Forget it."

"Do you think it was easy for us to go through with it?" Holly asked.

Staring at her friend, Mary saw the concern on her face.

"When Duke first told me about it, I didn't want to. I had to talk to Mom first."

Sheila patted her leg. "You don't have to do it. You'll be an old lady to the club, but it wouldn't be the same for them. Pike will never force you."

"I just can't stand to have them laughing at me."

"They'd never laugh at you. It doesn't leave the club, honey. It's purely part of the club. It's not to be scoffed at, laughed at, or talked about." Sheila smiled. "It's a club thing. Pike, it means something to him."

Mary closed the magazine she was reading. If it meant something to Pike then she was going to do it. For their wedding he was stepping out of his comfort zone. It was the least she could do.

"Could you take me to the clubhouse?" Mary asked.

"I can do that."

Holly stayed behind as Mary climbed into Sheila's car. She was doing the right thing. She knew she was and wouldn't regret a second of it.

****

Pike smacked the ball, watching as Daisy groaned.

"I win, pay up," Pike said, placing the pool stick in the corner.

"Damn, man, I remember when I could beat you."

"What can I say? No one can beat me." He took the money from Daisy, pocketing the cash.

"Oh, now that looks like trouble," Daisy said, looking over Pike's shoulder. The sound of the clubhouse door closing had Pike turning around. Mary stood there, glancing around. When she saw him, she moved toward him.

Stepping toward her, he wrapped his arms around her. "Hey, baby, I didn't know you were coming here."

"Neither did I."

"What is it?" he asked, seeing the worry in her eyes. They were getting married next month. He wasn't ready for her to quit on him.

"I'm sorry. I've been so selfish and mean. I want to give you what all the old ladies gave their men. I trust and love you, Pike. I want you, all of you, more than anything." His cock went from flaccid to hard within seconds. She ran her hand down his body. "I don't have to like it, but I love you, Pike. This is what I want. This is what it means to be your old lady completely."

"Are you sure?" He wasn't going to pretend he didn't know what she was talking about.

Duke was already clearing out the club whores. Russ left the room, and the men gave a wide berth to the couple.

"I know I love you. I'm sure of that, and I trust you." She cupped his cock, rubbing her fingers along his length. "I'm ready for this. I've been thinking about it for a long time. This isn't a quick decision for me."

He glanced toward the room, looking at the men. "Look at them, Mary. They wouldn't hurt you, and they will not talk about it. What happens in this room, stays in this room."

"Kind of like Vegas."

"No, this is better than Vegas. You won't even have to live with the consequences when it's over."

He moved her back toward the pool table. The balls were gone, and the table was clear. Pike didn't wait for the men to be ready. He didn't care about if they saw or not. All he cared about was the woman in his arms. Mary wore a yellow summer dress with small straps over her shoulders. He lifted her up, stepping between her thighs.

"This is my old lady. Anyone comes close and I swear to God, I will kill each and every one of you." He spoke the words clear for all to hear, not looking away from Mary. Pike ran his fingers up the inside of her thighs, teasing her. "You forget about them, Mary. Forget about the room and focus all on me. All I'm focused on is you. I don't give a fuck who sees that I love you."

He pushed her dress up, touching her core. Her panties were soaked.

"Or maybe not. Are you getting off being watched?"

"Shut up, Pike." She wrapped her arms around his neck, pulling him down. "You're the only one I'm wet for."

Releasing his cock, Pike stroked over his shaft as she teased him with her kisses. From his back pocket he pulled out a condom.

"You don't have to wear that. I'm on the pill. I'm not ready for children yet. I want to enjoy you before we bring kids into the mix."

For him, the whole club fell away. "I love you, Mary."

"And I love you, future husband."

Tugging her panties out of the way, he pocketed the fabric, groaning out as her slick pussy took his fingers. She cried out, keeping open for him. Her eyes were closed. Glancing around the room, he saw the respect in the men's eyes. They were watching, accepting Mary as his woman into the club. Duke nodded his head, clearly happy with the situation. This was what it meant to be part of the club and to claim an old lady. No one would touch her, hurt or abuse her. Mary was protected and would be loved by the club. Staring down at his woman, Pike knew Mary was a special person to him and to the club. She was Holly's best friend, and Russ considered her a daughter. Now, she was his old lady. The club recognized her as his and would take care of her like his property should be.

"They're watching us, baby. They know who you belong to, and they also know who I belong to." He claimed her lips before she could protest. Pike pinched and stroked her clit, watching her response to him. Mary opened her eyes, the love shining in her brown depths clear for him to see.

"I love you, Pike."

He tugged her to the edge of the pool table. She lay back against the felt covering. He teased his cock through her slit. Her cream covered his cock. When he was at the entrance to her clit, they stared at each other, and he sank inside her.

Mary cried out, arching up. Her gaze went around the room, taking in all of the men, watching them. None of them touched themselves, and Pike appreciated it. Mary was a nervous woman, yet with his dick inside her, she looked more beautiful than ever before. His woman, his soon to be wife.

Slamming his cock inside her, everything else fell away as he made love to his woman, his old lady, his property.

"I love you, Mary. I love you so much."

She sat up, wrapping her arms around him, kissing him as he forged inside her. Her heat swamped him. The pleasure was unlike anything he'd ever felt. During the whole of his life, he'd never had a woman to call his own. In fact, there had never been anything in his life that he called his own.

"I love you, baby. You're my heart, my soul, my life."

She cried out, speaking words of love.

Pike finally knew what it was to love one woman, to be with her completely. No one else would ever compare to her. He loved her more than anything.

He stroked over her clit, bringing her to orgasm as he found his own, in her arms, in front of the club, for life. If anything happened to him, the club would protect her, always. Pike knew he could sleep easier in the future with the club at his back with Mary.

When it was over, he glanced around the club before looking down at his woman. She was smiling up at him. "That wasn't too bad," she said.

Pike chuckled. "Speak for yourself. They didn't see you with an orgasm face."

She started laughing. The tightening of her pussy around his dick made him groan. Mary was perfect in every way. He'd never, ever take her for granted.

Epilogue

"Open wide," Mary said.

"I keep eating all of this cake and I'm going to end up fat," Pike said, opening his mouth to take more of the frosted chocolate cake. It was the town picnic, and the whole town was out to enjoy the fair, the food, including the club. Across from them Duke sat with Matthew and a heavily pregnant Holly. Everything was going right with Holly's pregnancy.

"I'll help you work off the cake later." She raised a brow, tempting him.

They'd been married for two months, and it was now summer. The tourists were passing through town enjoying the day at Vale Valley.

"Yum, that's your best yet." Mary had set up her cooking blog, and every day he was trying new recipes from her. She still worked at the diner, and he'd seen Mac with her. The two were clearly good friends, and he didn't want to change that. She wasn't giving him a break in anyway, and he didn't mind. She had stopped going to the gym, which he was thankful for. He noticed she still insisted on healthy eating. Pike loved seeing the happiness in her eyes and wouldn't do anything to jeopardize that. He'd do anything for her. Wrapping his arm around her waist, he took hold of her hand. He stared at their locked fingers seeing their wedding bands together.

She was all his, and he was all hers. Nothing was ever going to tear them apart. He wasn't going to back out of his word. Pike would never betray her. He loved her more than life itself.

Duke's words were exactly right, only he changed it up. Once he found the right woman that he wanted to fuck, love, and spend every waking moment with, he'd know. Mary, she was that woman.

The End

www.samcrescent.wordpress.com

SAM CRESCENT

Evernight Publishing

www.evernightpublishing.com